Second Chance Girl

A Novel

ALSO BY JESSICA THORN

• • • •

Pine Grove Romance Series

Christmas in Pine Grove

• • • •

Rocky Point Romance Series

Second Chance Girl
Just My Luck (Coming 2021)

• • • •

All Jessica Thorn's books can be read in Kindle Unlimited

Second Chance Girl

A Novel

. . . .

By Jessica Thorn

Any references to historical events, real people, or real places are used fictitiously. Names, characters, and places are products of the author's imagination.

Front cover image by germancreative

Printed by Kindle Direct Publishing, in the United States of America.

First printing edition 2020.

Second
Chance
Girl

A Novel

Chapter One

Elizabeth

"I SHOULD HAVE KNOWN you'd find a way to get rid of me, rotten girl."

I roll my eyes as I push my grandmother's wheelchair forward, through the front doors of Golden Acres Assisted Living. A chipper nurse in yellow scrubs gives us a sweet smile when she sees us, shaking my hand and waving at Gran.

"Elizabeth Quinn," I tell her, and then gesture to Gran. "This is my grandmother."

"You must be Helen," she coos, addressing Gran. "I'm nurse Angie, I'm here to help you get settled."

"I'll be settled when I'm dead."

The nurse's smile falters for a moment, her eyes widening and flicking toward me. I shrug, patting Gran on the shoulder.

"You're going to like it here," I tell her, noting I don't sound all too convincing. "Remember the tour you took with Cheryl? You said you really liked the apartment."

"I only said that because Cheryl liked it," Gran tells me.

"Ahh, of course," I say, briefly squeezing my eyes shut. "I forgot we're only agreeable with Cheryl."

Gran pauses for a moment, a smile crossing her face at the mention of her caretaker of four years. "I don't like to upset Cheryl."

Right, I thought. *Just me, apparently.*

Angie beckons us forward, leading us through the large lobby and toward a common area, with tables and a television. It's barely 9 a.m., but a handful of other residents are already gathering in the common area, sipping on coffee and tea, and quietly watching QVC, playing cards, or reading. We stop for a moment and Gran turns to me, the disappointment in her eyes reminding me of the way she used to look at me when I'd talk back to her as a kid, or when she'd catch me sneaking out in the middle of the night as a teenager.

"Ungrateful, rotten child."

Angie's head snaps toward me, the surprise in her eyes tinged with a hint of panic. I pat Gran's shoulder again, smiling at Angie.

"Your apartment is just down this way," Angie mutters, leading us down a hallway at the other end of the common area. She stops outside a door marked with the number six, turns the handle, and opens the door into Gran's unit.

I roll her in and help her take her coat off, then hang it on the coat rack by the door. Cheryl had helped move in some of Gran's things the week before, and I had unpacked what I could last night, before moving Gran in this morning. Despite the touches from home scattered throughout the apartment, the space still has a detached and rather, well... *depressing* feel to it.

"Alright, Gran, what do you think?" I ask, walking around to stand in front of her. "Want me to help you onto the couch?"

Gran looks up at me, cocks her head to the side, and smiles widely at me.

"You have such beautiful hair, dear," she says, then looks around the room. "Is this your house?"

I frown, crouching down in front of her. She follows me with her eyes, and something about them unsettles me. They're glassy and uncertain, full of a twinkling innocence that is almost childlike. Not a hint of her usual ire toward me, not even the faintest bit of recognition, registers in her gaze.

"Gran?" I say, rubbing her arm. "It's me, Elizabeth."

"That's a beautiful name, dear."

I drop my head, inhaling a deep breath, and then stand up. Angie gives me a sympathetic nod, walking over and grasping the handles on Gran's wheelchair.

"Her doctor sent over the dosage for her medications, so I'll get those together for her. You take a moment," she says, wheeling Gran into her bedroom. Once they are both out of eyesight, I exhale, rubbing my forehead. Cheryl had told me what had been going on with her recently – the forgetting, the confusion, and the speech disruptions. I'd spoken with her doctor, and she'd explained to me the symptoms and outlook of dementia. She classified Gran as having middle stage, or moderate dementia, and assured me it would only continue to get more severe as time went on. An assisted living facility with a memory care unit for when things got bad would be the best option for her condition, despite Gran's complaints. I knew what to expect, but... it still caught me off guard seeing it happen in front of my eyes. The forgetting, that is.

A few hours later, with Gran settled and taking her afternoon nap, I decide now is as good a time as ever to work on the thing I am least looking forward to during my short return to my hometown of Rocky Point: figuring out what in the world to do with Gran's house. With Angie promising to check in on Gran frequently, I head out into the balmy summer afternoon, climb into my Lexus (a rental, so why not splurge?), and take off toward Rocky Point proper and the past I left behind some ten odd years ago.

• • • •

DRIVING INTO TOWN FEELS like teleporting back in time, the neatly lined blocks of Cape Cod-style houses, the blue expanse of the harbor, and the towering silhouette of the light house all achingly familiar. On the water, I can see sailboats tacking and jibing with the wind, the occasional larger yacht moseying in between them. It's Saturday, and the streets are cluttered with townies and tourists alike, hitting the shops on Main Street or grabbing a bite at the local haunts. I think of Crabby Jack's, my favorite place to get crab legs or a buttery Lobster Roll as a kid, and smile. I'll have to try to stop by while I'm in town.

I don't have to navigate to get to Gran's house, despite not having been back in close to a decade. I know the drive like the back of my hand. As I pull into the driveway, though, and put the Lexus in park, I look around at the yard and frown. The crisp, manicured front lawn that I remember is now brown and overgrown. The tulips that once lined the walkway leading up to the house are wilted and frail, nothing like their former vibrant and colorful selves. The exterior of the house, in my memory a robin's egg blue Cape Cod with navy shutters, has paint peeling off the siding and moss growing on the aging gray roof. I remember Gran's meticulous gardening and upkeep of the space as a child, and am overcome with a momentary wave of sadness. I slept in a hotel last night, meeting Cheryl at the nursing home to pick up Gran this morning. I had purposely put off this moment, worrying about what it would be like to see my childhood home again, and wondering if I could somehow just *skip* it entirely. It's worse that I could have anticipated.

Carefully, I climb out of the car and make the short trek up to the front door, pulling out the worn brass key and sticking it in the lock. I hesitate, inhaling a deep breath before turning the key and pushing the door open. The hardwood floor creaks as I step inside, and as I take a look around, I realize it's not half as bad as the outside. In fact, everything looks strangely... *preserved?* Like no one has sat on the furniture in years. A thick layer of dust coats almost everything, and all the curtains on the windows are drawn tightly shut. I throw them open, one by one, to let some light in. Storm clouds have begun to roll in, so it's not very bright, but even the tiny bit of natural light makes the house come just slightly back to life.

As I stroll through the house, it feels like a time capsule, everything exactly the same as when I left ten years ago. I make my way upstairs, instinctively skipping the squeaky third stair from the top landing, and stopping in front of the closed door at the end of the hallway. My old bedroom. Just as I reach for the doorknob, a loud crack of thunder shakes the house and I jump, closing my eyes as the sound of driving rain gets louder and louder.

Not yet, my brain practically yells. *We're not ready yet.*

I back away from the door, figuring there's no reason to check out my old bedroom *quite* yet.

Chicken shit, I think.

I take a few more steps back, turning around to head downstairs again, when a big, fat drop of water hits me square in the center of my forehead. I freeze, the out-of-place and unexpected feeling of being rained on causing my brain to grasp for its bearings. I look up, toward the source of the droplets, and gasp at a large, yellow ring on the ceiling the size of a dinner plate. Water drips from the center of the ring, the dripping becoming faster and faster as the rain outside continues to drive louder and harder against the house.

"Crap!" I yell, bolting downstairs to look for a bucket or large bowl. I find a bucket under the kitchen sink and grab several towels from the linen closet, silently thanking Cheryl for not packing *everything* up. I spread the towels out in the hallway underneath the leaking ceiling, and plant the bucket under the stream of droplets, flinching as I feel another drop of water hit my back. Looking up, I see another yellow ring, and another stream of droplets. Scanning the rest of the hallway, I see a handful of other damp spots beginning to form. *Damn.*

Dashing out to my car, I climb in and type *hardware store* into the GPS app on my phone, sighing with relief when it returns one close by that's still open. A few minutes later, I pull up in front of Dearing's Hardware, a small mom-and-pop shop that I remember well from my childhood. Back when I was in school, the shop was run by Charlie Dearing, the father of a classmate of mine. Eddie Dearing had been a quiet, loner-type kid, taking after his tall and portly father at a young age. I remember the popular kids teasing him mercilessly. As I hurry out of my car, soaked through from the rain, I wonder if Eddie runs the store now.

A bell chimes as I clamber through the door, shaking off the rain on the mat in the vestibule before stepping onto the store's linoleum floor. A petite blonde woman in light wash overalls over a white t-shirt bounces out from behind the counter to greet me, but gasps after taking one look at me.

"I know, I'm positively sopping," I sigh.

"Lizzie? Lizzie Quinn?"

My head snaps up at the sound of my nickname – one I haven't gone by since I left Rocky Point. I squint at the woman, not recognizing her right away. Her face is familiar, but perhaps less heavily made up? Finally, the lightbulb goes off. Her hair is different, much shorter now. What used to be enviable golden waves down to her hips is now a platinum, wavy, chin-length bob. She is smiling at me, the same brilliant straight, white smile she would flash on the football field before being hurled into the air during a cheer routine.

"Trisha Dodd?"

Trisha squeals excitedly when I recognize her.

"Yes! Oh my *gosh*, what's it been? 10 years?" The way she clasps her hands and bounces up and down on her toes, I'm worried she's about to do a back handspring.

"Just about," I say.

"Well, it sure is good to see you. You haven't changed one bit! Except for maybe that coat," she gestures to my tan Michael Kors trench. "That looks *expensive*."

I don't know how to respond, so I just smile.

I'm unnerved by how *different* Trisha is. When we were in school together, she was at the top of the food chain, second only to head cheerleader Ainsley Wells. I distinctly remember her wearing her Mean Girl badge with pride. The Trisha Dodd of high school wouldn't have been caught dead talking to me, let alone thinking it's good to see me. *Or* wearing overalls.

"So, what can I help you find?" she asks, pointing to her nametag. "I'm Trisha *Dearing* now, by the way. Can you believe it?"

I can feel my eyes bulging out of my sockets. "No, I can't," I say flatly. Trisha Dodd and Eddie Dearing? I consider hitting myself with a nearby object, just to see if I'm awake, because surely, I *must* be hallucinating. When I look around, however, the only objects at arms' length are buy-one-get-one hand trowels and gardening spades, both of which would no doubt get me sent to the nearest psych ward if I started flailing them around. Instead, I look at Trisha and smile.

"I'm looking for some buckets. And a large plastic tarp," I say. She cocks her head to one side, and I add, "Oh, and potentially some sandbags, if you have them."

Trisha bursts out into giggles.

"My goodness, Lizzie Quinn. You haven't gone and murdered someone, have you?"

I exhale sharply. "Nope, just have a leaky roof."

"Oh, well that's never fun!" Trisha says, leading me toward an aisle with several bucket varieties. I grab a few off the shelf, and then she takes me to the next aisle over for a tarp. "I know someone who could come take a look at the roof for you, if you want."

"Oh Trisha, that would be great, actually," I say, hauling a few sandbags into the buckets. "I'm supposed to be deciding whether or not to sell the house, but there's no way I can do that if the roof needs replaced."

"Selling?" Trisha asks. "Your Gran's place? Is Helen okay?"

I look down at my sopping wet ballet flats. "We had to move her into Golden Acres. She's been..." I hesitate, not sure I trust Trisha enough to blab personal family business. "On the decline."

"Oh no, I'm so sorry to hear that!" Trisha gushes. "Listen, I know a handyman who owes me a favor. I'll have him head to Helen's as soon as we're finished here to get you an estimate."

"Thanks so much, Trisha."

She rings me out, and lets me know to expect her handyman in thirty to forty-five minutes, tops. "And let's get coffee sometime soon, catch up!" she yells, waving after me as I lug what I've bought back out into the still-pounding rain. I smile at her and nod. *So weird.*

A few minutes later, I pull back into Gran's driveway and haul the buckets, tarp, and sandbags inside in one trip. I strip off my rain-soaked jacket and blouse, leaving just my damp tank top and jeans clinging to my skin, and kick off my water-logged flats. I run upstairs and dry off any wet spots on the floor, then spread out the buckets under the leaks. Just as I'm finishing up, I hear a knock on the front door.

That was quick, I think to myself, making a mental note to thank Trisha again.

"Come on in, door's open!" I yell, double checking that I have all the leaks covered. I hear the door creak open downstairs, and then close with a *thud.* "I'll be right down!"

I pad downstairs to greet the handyman Trisha has sent over, preparing to rattle off the location of the leaks, when I see the man standing in my foyer and freeze, nearly tripping down the last couple steps.

Cameron Tate. My high school sweetheart.

He's leaning against the door, his gray t-shirt and jeans soaked through to the bone. The dampness of his shirt causes it to cling to the broad, defined muscles in his chest and shoulders, and the glistening droplets of water on his skin accentuate the dark bronze color, no doubt from countless hours of labor in the sun. Any other day, any other world, I would be overjoyed to find a tall, muscular, soaking wet man in my entryway. Right now, though, I'm panicking. I want my entire body to dry up and shrivel into nothingness, kind of like my throat is doing. If there was ever a time for a pit of quicksand to appear and swallow me whole, it's now.

"Lizzie."

He says my name so low, it's practically a growl. I attempt to speak, but my mouth is so dry I feel like I've just stuffed it full of cotton. He crosses his arms over his chest and waits while I conduct a full reset of my brain. *Systems... processing...*

"C...Cam," I stutter. *Doing great, champ.* "What are you doing here?"

I feel like a total idiot the moment the question leaves my stupid mouth. It's now that I realize he's wearing a tool belt. He cocks one eyebrow, and the familiarity of that look, even if it's been a decade, sends a shiver down my spine.

"I'm here to look at your roof."

Chapter Two

Elizabeth

I STAND THERE LIKE a dunce, my left foot hovering over the next step down, my mouth slightly agape. Cam is looking at me like he's concerned I've had a stroke, and I can see his hand twitching toward his cell phone, probably ready to dial 911.

Yes, emergency services? I think she keeled over from embarrassment.

"You're here to look at the roof," I repeat, causing Cam's eyebrows to shoot upward.

"Yes. Trisha sent me. Said it was an emergency."

Trisha. Maybe not so much has changed after all.

I inhale a deep breath, hoping to send enough oxygen to my brain cells that they'll start functioning normally again. It helps, a bit.

"When she said handyman, she didn't really specify *which* handyman," I say, and he makes a face like I punched him in the gut. *Elizabeth, get it together.*

"I see."

"Not that I mind that it's you," I continue, figuring I already dug myself a hole, better to just toss myself in it already. "It's really nice to see you, Cam."

He doesn't say anything. I can tell it's not nice to see me.

"Where's Helen?" he asks, looking around the dark and dusty sitting room.

"Golden Acres Assisted Living," I tell him, and his face falls. "Dementia."

I don't know why I tell him that last part. I guess some part of me must still trust him, not that he'd ever given me a reason not to. He also knows Gran better than most.

"Show me where the leak is at," he says curtly, not making eye contact. I turn around to go back up the steps, gesturing for him to follow me.

"I'm doing swell, thanks for asking," I mutter, just loud enough so he can hear me. I hear him snicker between the loud thuds of his shoes on the staircase. When we get to the top landing, I spread my arms wide toward the ceiling. "The leaks. As in, several of them."

He gets to work inspecting them, brushing past me like I'm some sort of obstacle in his way. He grabs a roll of measuring tape off of his tool belt and takes measurements of the stains on the ceiling, not saying a damn word.

"So, you work construction now?" I ask, trying to make conversation. He snorts.

"I own a contracting business in town," he says, still focused entirely on the ceiling.

"That's great," I say, and I mean it. Growing up, Cam always wanted to make his own way in the world. By the looks of things, he'd accomplished that.

"It's no swanky office job in the big city, but I get by," he says, and it hurts exactly the way he intends it to. When I look to the floor, not saying anything, he adds, "I'm sorry about Helen. I know she loves you very much, even if she has a funny way of showing it."

You loved me very much too, once.

The thought hits me unexpectedly, and I recoil visibly. Cam just shakes his head, laughing.

"What's so funny?" I ask, annoyed at how *defensive* I sound. *Why does he still make me feel like a nervous teenager?*

He whips out his cell phone and starts snapping pictures of the leaky ceiling. "I can just see you still live inside your head, is all."

I take it as a challenge.

"We should grab drinks sometime," I say, channeling my fiercest badass so that I don't head screaming for the hills. "Catch up."

He pockets his phone, snorts a laugh, and then heads downstairs. Confused, and honestly a little bruised in the ego department, I race after him.

"Or would your girlfriend mind?" I ask, and when he doesn't respond, add, "Or wife?"

He messes with his phone again, quickly typing what appears to be a text message with the photos of Gran's ceiling attached.

"Boyfriend?" I ask skeptically, and he finally whips his head up to meet my gaze. His denim blue eyes burn as they bear into my own, boiling over with an emotion I can't quite place. If I didn't know any better, I would think he's in pain.

"No," he says, his voice as sharp as a knife. In an instant, the distance between us shortens by a good six inches, and he's right in front of me. I don't know who moved, him or I, but it doesn't matter. I suddenly can't breathe, and want to kick myself over how awkward it would be if I just passed out in front of Cam right here, right now.

"No girlfriend. No wife," he says, and is it just me? Or does his suddenly sound huskier? I can feel my cheeks flush, and he smirks. "No boyfriend."

He takes a giant step backward, opens the front door, and steps out onto the porch.

"I'll have one of my guys come over and assess the roof when it stops raining," he says. "He'll determine if it can be patched, or if it needs replacing."

"One of your guys?" I ask, still a little breathless and scrambled in the brains. "Not you?"

"I have a business to run. That's why I pay my crew, to work."

It makes sense, but for some reason my mouth still wants to protest.

"Is that a no to drinks, then?" I ask.

His face reveals absolutely nothing.

"I'll send someone over first thing in the morning, weather permitting," he says. "Have a nice life, Lizzie."

I watch him dash out into the rain and climb into his black Ford pickup truck, not bothering to take even one more glance my way. For reasons I can't quite make heads or tails of, I feel like I'm going to cry.

• • • •

ROCKY POINT, MASSACHUSETTS. May 2010
   10 years earlier
   Something has felt off all day, but I *know* something is wrong when Cam doesn't show up to our spot at Java Point after school. I type out my billionth text in the last ten minutes, fingers trembling, and hit 'send'.

   Pls talk 2 me Cam. Where r u?

   In my gut, I know why he's ignoring me. After class, I had excitedly told Ms. Sable, our graphic arts teacher, about how I'd gotten into N.Y.U's Advertising Program after being waitlisted. She'd written me a recommendation, so I *had* to thank her, obviously. When I left, though, I noticed Ainsley Wells creeping by the door, listening to every single word we had said. I watched her eyes light up, the way any mean girl's does when they're about to ruin someone's life. When she slithered off, I knew it wouldn't be good.

   I haven't told Cam that I'm leaving yet. I figure Ainsley took care of that.

   To be fair, I only *just* decided to go to N.Y.U. I have been trying to figure out how to tell him for like four days, and had been planning to today at Java Point over a caramel frappe. Until *Ainsley* ruined everything.

   I jump as my phone buzzes, whipping it out of my pocket, eyes glued to the screen. *It's him!*

   Be there soon.

Well, it's better than nothing, I think.

   Those three words would normally set my heart galloping at light speed. Just the thought of seeing Cam generally made me feel a mixture of nervousness, giddiness, and desire like I'd never felt with anyone else. I never wanted to be with someone the way I wanted to be with Cam. Today, though... the thought of him walking through the door makes me feel like I want to hurl.

I purchase two caramel frappes, grab our usual seat by the window, and wait, my leg bobbing nervously up and down. By the time Cam arrives, I've already sucked down 90% of my frappe and I feel on the verge of tears.

Cam strolls into Java Point with his most laid back, cool-guy-face on. It's the same expression he wears when he's out with his football team, or getting lectured by his teacher, and only I know that it's a façade. I know that it's Cam's way of hiding his feelings, whether he's sad, or mad, or disappointed, to just pretend like he doesn't care. This is the first time he's ever used that face with me.

He's wearing his Rocky Point High football t-shirt, which declares him the team Captain. His dirty blond hair is messy and adorable, curling up at the nape of his neck and around his ears. His blue eyes look directly into mine, and I can see the sadness in them – the sadness I caused.

"Cam," I start, reaching across the table to grab his hands in mine. I've always been more of a visual person, and words haven't always come super naturally to me. Right now, they are failing me. "I got into N.Y.U., they took me off waitlist."

He takes a moment before saying, "That's great, Lizzie. I'm happy for you."

His tone is halfhearted at best. "It doesn't sound like you're very happy for me," I say, and he shakes his head.

"I am, really," he says. "I'm just disappointed you'll be so far away is all. And I'm pissed I had to hear it from Ainsley, and not from you."

I lean back and fold my arms across my chest. "You weren't supposed to hear it from *Ainsley*," I seethe. "She overheard me talking to Ms. Sable, and probably figured this was her chance."

"Her chance to what?"

I roll my eyes because it's *so* obvious. "Steal you away, duh."

He runs a hand through his hair. "Ainsley isn't trying to steal me away from you, Lizzie. She was trying to be a good friend."

"Right, she's always just trying to be a *good friend*. She just always happens to get involved when she should mind her own business."

I know for certain that Ainsley Wells doesn't care about being a good friend. If I had to guess, Ainsley cares about three things, tops: boys, makeup, and making everyone around her miserable. Cam has always been blind to Ainsley's mean girl ways, though. As head cheerleader, Ainsley has always thought that Cam is *hers*, and hers only. So, when he started dating me, a quiet, definitely-not-popular girl, it drove her absolutely crazy. I'm pissed that she still is trying to get between us, even with high school being practically over.

"Still, you should have told me first," he says. I can't fault him there.

"I know, I'm sorry."

"I don't get why N.Y.U. is so important. Can't you major in advertising at like, any school?"

"Because if I want to *be somebody* in advertising, I have to go somewhere like N.Y.U. I can't do that in Rocky Point," I explain, for what feels like the millionth time. "I know you're happy to stay here and go to trade school, and that's fine! But that's just not what I want. I need to go make something of myself."

"You don't think I'll make something of myself staying here?" he asks, the hurt slicing through his voice like a blade.

"I didn't mean it like that," I backtrack. "I just mean... you know what happened to my parents. I can't let that happen to me."

"Yeah, because *all* people who don't go to college turn into felons and drug addicts. Come on, Lizzie."

I bite back tears, the curt words about my mother and father feeling like knives ripping at barely healed scabs over deep, dark wounds. We sit in silence for a few minutes, Cam sipping at his now melted drink while I stare out the window. Finally, I murmur, "What about a long-distance relationship? We could make it work, Cam."

"I don't know, Lizzie. You're going to meet all new people, have a whole new life. You'll forget about me," he says.

"No I won't!" I insist, wanting to launch myself across the little table and into his arms. "I couldn't forget about you Cam."

He lifts his eyes, now cold and hard as steel, to mine. "It's not going to work, Lizzie. If you're going to N.Y.U. then I think..."

"You think what?" I'm crying now, more because his face lacks any trace of emotion than because of what I think he's implying.

"If you go to N.Y.U., then I think that's it."

Ice courses through my veins. He's not even willing to try? He's going to give me an ultimatum, just like that? I resolve to myself that, if he cared for me at all, he wouldn't make me pick between him or my dreams. He would do everything he could to make this work, from wherever either of us ended up. If he's not willing to do that, then he must not care about me at all.

"Fine," I say through gritted teeth, standing up from my chair and pushing it in gently. "Then I guess that's it."

He doesn't look up at me, instead keeping his eyes fixed on the wall across from him. I grab my backpack off the floor, using every ounce of willpower I have not to beg him to change his mind, not to throw myself at him and cry into his shoulder like I so desperately want to. Instead, I turn around and walk out of the coffee shop, waiting until I'm at least a few blocks away before I let myself cry.

I don't look back.

Chapter Three

Cameron

WHAT. THE. *Fuck.*

I sit in the driveway of my house, truck still running, waiting for my pulse to slow down and my breathing to get back under control.

She's here. Like, *here.* In Rocky Point. Ten years without a word and suddenly she shows up out of nowhere, like she was just willed into existence. When Trisha asked me to do her a favor and head over to a house nearby to check out their leaking roof, I couldn't have imagined that would mean running into Elizabeth Quinn again. Honestly, I hadn't even seen her grandmother since Elizabeth left town, the woman mostly kept to herself. Rocky Point isn't the biggest town in Cape Cod, but it isn't so small that you can't be anonymous if you want to. I should know, seeing as I spent a good few years keeping to myself after...

Shit.

And the way Trisha said it, like she felt sorry for me or something. *It's Helen Quinn's house. Just so you know... Lizzie is there. I thought you should know.*

The pity in her voice, like she was worried I might crumble at the news, killed me. What was worse? I very well might have. It took every ounce of willpower, the strength of every fiber of every muscle in my body, to remain emotionless at the sight of Lizzie Quinn.

Lizzie had looked beautiful, too. Her blonde hair was shorter than she'd worn it in high school, falling just below her shoulders in perfect, golden waves. Her jeans still hugged the generous curves of her hips and thighs, driving me absolutely, categorically insane. The only difference was the dark circles under her amber eyes, like months of stress and sleepless nights were weighing on her. The stress of her grandmother's illness must be taking a toll, even though she and Helen have never had that close of a relationship. What really did me in, though, was the way she looked at me. The surprise in her eyes – Trisha obviously hadn't told her who she'd called – mixed with the slightest hint of... excitement? Was I making that up? She *had* asked if I wanted to catch up sometime. And like an idiot, I blew her off.

It would be a bad idea, anyway. What would be the point? Our paths diverged a long time ago, no sense in trying to force anything.

I shut off my truck and climb out, realizing that there's another car in my driveway. I had been too wrapped up in my thoughts when I pulled in to see it earlier, but the shiny red SUV tells me that my mother has stopped by to pay me a visit. As I amble up the walkway to my front porch, I can see her sitting on the porch swing, her little Shih Tzu, Bella, vibrating anxiously on her lap. She stands when she sees me and leaves Bella on the swing, wrapping me in a hug.

"Hey, mom."

"Cameron, my favorite son," she says with a wink.

"Don't let Gray here you say that," I chuckle. Grayson, my baby brother, has always maintained that he is my mother's favorite son. I think, secretly, she tells us we both are.

"If Grayson was so concerned about being my favorite son, he wouldn't have moved to California."

"You'll feel differently when he's famous," I say, causing her to smile. After my dad died of a heart attack a few years back, Gray moved to Los Angeles to pursue a career in acting. Mom hadn't wanted him to go so far away, but I knew he needed to go in order to heal. For me, healing meant taking over the family business and fulfilling dad's dreams. For Gray, it meant getting out of dodge.

"So, to what do I owe this surprise visit?" I ask, opening the front door and ushering mom and Bella inside. I fill up a small bowl with water and set it on the ground for Bella while my mom takes a seat at my long, farmhouse-style kitchen table. She smooths her hands over the freshly stained wood, something I just got around to doing last week. I'd refinished both the table and the six chairs that came with it after finding the table sitting carelessly on the side of the road, worn and scratched and headed for the dump. With a little love, it turned out to be the perfect addition to my large, eat-in kitchen that I'd finished renovating a few months ago.

"I'm glad you finally have a kitchen table, sweetie, but don't you think this is a bit big for one person?" she asks. I narrow my eyes at her. Where is she going with this?

"I think it fits the space perfectly," I say. "The dark, natural finish on the wood complements the stark white cabinets and quartz countertops, don't you think?"

The kitchen is actually the part of this house I'm most proud of. I bought the house just over a year ago during a foreclosure sale. The place was a wreck, but slowly I'd renovated every single inch of the place. I'd saved the kitchen for last, since I rarely spent time in the kitchen anyway, but had been extremely proud of how modern and inviting it had turned out.

"It's a beautiful kitchen," she agrees. "Just seems like it might be missing a woman's touch, is all."

Ah. There it is.

My mother has been not-so-subtly dropping hints about her feelings toward my love life, or *lack thereof,* since I bought the house. Recently, she's started to up her game by complaining about her lack of grandchildren, and her years of being able to spoil them slowly wasting away.

I roll my eyes at her. "Mom, we've talked about this. No amount of guilt-tripping is going to make me married with kids any faster."

She gasps, a hand flying to her chest while mischief dances in her eyes. "I'm hurt! Do you really think I'd guilt trip my own son into getting married so I can have lots of grandbabies to keep me busy? The thought!"

"Uh huh."

She crosses her arms, the twinkling in her eyes only growing stronger.

"Well from what I hear, I may not have to guilt you. Fate might do that for me."

The hairs on the back of my neck stand on end as I take in my mother's sly smile.

"What do you mean by that?" I ask, the gruffness in my voice no deterrent to her meddling.

"I heard that a certain someone is back in town."

So much for anonymity.

"How'd you hear that? I only just found out myself," I say.

"Betty Grabis saw her at Helen's early today, and told Phyllis Weitzman at the Bridge Club that meets at the Senior Center on Saturday mornings," she says. "I ran into Phyllis when I went to the grocery store just a little while ago, and wanted to come tell you."

"Well, you're too late because I already know."

"How'd *you* find out?" she asks.

"I went to take a look at her roof."

My mom's mouth drops open, as if I'd just given her the best news all year.

"You *saw* her?" she asks, causing me to roll my eyes again.

"Yes," I say. "What's the big deal?"

Mom stands and walks around to me, patting me on the shoulder. There it is, that *pity* again. Before I know it, the whole town will probably be giving me sullen looks and sending me sympathy cards.

"The big deal is that Elizabeth Quinn was your first *love*, Cameron. Your only love, as far as I can tell. It must be difficult to see her again."

"I appreciate your concern, mom, but I'm fine."

"Are you going to see her again?" she asks.

"What? No way," I say, shaking my head. "I'll send some guys to help patch up Helen's roof, but I'm not going anywhere near Elizabeth. All of that is in the past."

She sighs heavily before returning to her seat at the table, looking downright disappointed. I can feel myself beginning to get annoyed, as much as I hate to feel that way about my own mother. I just don't want or need her butting in, is all. Not with this.

"I just think you didn't give her a fair chance, is all," she says. I clench my jaw, trying not to let the anger bubbling up inside of me rear its ugly head. "She went to college, a perfectly normal thing for an 18-year-old girl to do, and you didn't want to give a long-distance relationship a shot. I know it hurt you that she went so far away, but you were both *kids*, Cameron. You didn't even give it a chance."

"Mom, I'm not having this conversation," I say firmly. In my mother's typical fashion, she ignores me.

"Why don't you just try to talk to her? What can that hurt?"

I stand up abruptly from my seat and grip the back of my neck. What can it hurt? Oh, I don't know. My heart. My pride. *Again.* I don't tell my mom this, though.

"You haven't had a serious relationship since Elizabeth," she continues. "I don't think you've ever gotten over her."

"Mom, enough. Okay?"

She raises her hands as if I'm pointing a gun at her. "Alright," she says. "I just want what's best for you, honey. I just want to see you happy."

"And I appreciate that," I say, my voice softening. "I just don't want to talk about this right now, okay?"

"Okay," she concedes. She looks around the kitchen again, taking in the white, custom cabinetry I built, the shiny quartz counter tops, and the wide, copper farmhouse sink. "It really is a beautiful house. Your father would be proud."

I smile, wishing my dad could be here to see my hard work. "Thanks, mom. I think so, too."

• • • •

A FEW HOURS LATER, I'm sitting in Ryan's Pub nursing a beer and a bad attitude. My mom didn't bring up Elizabeth again after I'd asked her to drop it, but the damage was done. She'd reminded me of the very thing I'd spent the last several years trying to forget: I let Lizzie get away.

I mean sure, she hadn't been as honest with me as she should have been about what school she'd picked. And yes, there were plenty of closer options. But she had still wanted to be with me, still wanted to try, and I'd given her an ultimatum – me, or college. What was she supposed to do, not go to college? Give up on her dreams? Asking her to throw it all away and stay in Rocky Point had been a selfish thing to do, but that's what I'd done. I'd been the one to make her choose. I couldn't blame her when she'd chosen what was best for her, even if it didn't include me.

A bell chimes above the door, and Eddie Dearing strolls into the bar, spotting me immediately. He makes a beeline toward me and plops down in the seat next to me at the bar. The bartender, Laura Jean, bounces over to us and gives Eddie a knowing smile.

"Bleu Cheese Burger and a Miller Lite?" she asks Eddie, who nods while she scribbles on her notepad. She gives him a wink. "Be right up."

Laura Jean makes it a point to memorize every regular customer's order. The minute I'd stepped into the bar, she'd had my usual Sam Adams lager on the counter waiting for me. She's worked at Ryan's Pub for as long as I can remember, long before her long brown hair turned silver and her attitude toward out-of-towner's and newly minted 21-year-old's had soured.

"So, Trish tells me you're doing some work for Lizzie Quinn," Eddie says, as Laura Jean slides him his beer.

"Words travels fast," I say, causing Eddie to snort a laugh.

"Have you forgotten who my wife is?" Eddie grins, and I nod. The man has a point. Before she was Trisha Dearing, Eddie's wife was Trisha Dodd, one of the It Girls of our high school and a notorious drama queen. It shouldn't come as a surprise that she wouldn't be too tight-lipped about the whole thing.

"I guess you're right."

"Well, happy to help you out with whatever materials you need. You just let me or Trish know." He tips his beer bottle toward me, I raise mine, and we clink bottles.

"Will do, man. Thanks."

I try to order my supplies and materials from Eddie as often as possible. I like to purchase locally whenever I can, and it's almost an unspoken rule in Rocky Point that local small business take precedence over the big box stores the next town over. Even if Eddie doesn't have something in stock, he's always willing to order it in for me, and my customer's usually don't mind being delayed a few days for the sake of supporting a local business owner.

"You know, between you and me, I think Trish might've been doing a little matchmaking when she called you earlier," Eddie says, taking another long pull from his beer.

"What makes you say that?"

"If she hadn't told you Lizzie was in town, would you have gone? Or would you have just sent one of your guys over to check it out?" he asks. And I have to admit, he has me there.

If Trisha hadn't told me about Lizzie being in town, I wouldn't have thought twice about sending one of my guys over to check it out. The moment I'd heard her name, though, it was like a light switch had been flipped. I told Trisha I would send someone out, but I'd been in my truck and on my way before she could even hang up. The truth was, I'd *needed* to see her myself. I needed closure, or something close. I needed to know that I could walk away from her on my own terms, so I could stop feeling like I'd thrown away the most magical thing in my life.

"If you want my opinion though," Eddie starts, removing his baseball cap and running a hand through his hair. I just shake my head.

"I don't."

Eddie continues on anyway. "I think you've just had a second chance drop right into your lap."

The thought had crossed my mind, but I'm not about to tell Eddie that. If seeing Lizzie had shown me anything, it's that she is still my Kryptonite, after all this time. No, this isn't a second chance. Not for me.

Chapter Four

Elizabeth

"MISS? ARE YOU SITTING here?"

I'm standing in Java Point, holding a large cup of coffee, and staring at the table by the front window when I feel someone tap me on the shoulder. I snap back to reality, and turn around to see an older couple holding coffees and pastries, pointing to the table.

"Are you sitting here?" the man asks again, and I shake my head.

"No, not at all. Sorry," I say, finding a small table far away from the window and parking my exhausted butt down before I totally lose it. I got maybe an hour or two of sleep, waking up what seemed like every two minutes in between dreams of Cam, and how we left things so long ago. Typically, coffee does the trick. Today, not so much.

I take a desperate sip, closing my eyes as I let the caffeine seep deep into my soul. When I open them, Trisha is sitting across from me, beaming. She's in a bright pink tank top and denim shorts, and looks a lot more like the Trisha I remember. I scowl when I see her.

"Hi!" she exclaims, smiling so wide I begin to wonder if her cheeks ever get tired.

"Hello," I say, avoiding eye contact as best as I can.

"I came in for a latte, and saw you sitting here. Figured I'd check in on how everything went with the roof last night."

If my eyes could shoot laser beams, I would burn a hole right through our little table. *Wishful thinking*. Instead, I turn them on Trisha.

"Peachy," I say. She claps her hands together, then gives me a conspiratorial wink.

"I have something to tell you," she says. I take another long draw from my coffee cup before acknowledging what she has said.

"And what's that?" I ask, wondering where on earth she could possibly be going with this.

"The handyman I called? Well... it was Cam."

I take another sip of my coffee, trying to figure out if I had just entered the Twilight Zone. "Yeah," I say. "I know."

"You *do?*" she asks, and now I can't help it. I glare at her, trying to figure out what kind of game she thinks she's playing right now.

"Obviously, Trisha. He showed up at the house."

Trisha screws up her face as she digests what I've just said. "Cam showed up at your house?" she asks.

"Are we having two separate conversations? Or..."

Suddenly, her mouth drops open like someone has just told her the juiciest secret ever. "Oh my *God,*" she says, slapping the table so hard I'm surprised it doesn't crumble beneath us. "He stopped by your *house!*"

Rather than answering, I take several more gulps of coffee. My lack of responsiveness, however, doesn't faze Trisha.

"I called him yesterday after you left and asked if he could send one of his guys over," Trisha explains. "I told him that I'd seen you, and that you needed someone to look at the roof. He told me he'd send one of his newbies over to take some measurements of the leak. I gave him the heads up because, well... your history and all... I didn't want any awkwardness."

"Well," I say, "mission *not* accomplished."

I feel like all the air has suddenly left my lungs. Trisha is still staring at me, practically vibrating with excitement.

"So, was that the first time you two have seen each other since...?"

Since I broke his heart and left town? "Yeah, it was."

Trisha reaches out and grabs my arm, and I freeze. I still can't get used to Trisha being a nice person, and yet, she's in front of me, living proof of a mean girl, reformed.

"Are you okay?" she asks. "How did that go?"

Deciding that what I need most in this moment is a friend, I tell Trisha everything.

She listens with rapt attention as I walk through my entire brief, yet slightly embarrassing, run in with Cam. When I finish, she is practically hysterical.

"You asked him out for drinks?" she asks, and I nod shamefully.

"And he declined. By practically sprinting out of the house."

She dissolves into hysterics again, and I playfully smack her on the arm.

"That's rough, babe," she says. "I wouldn't take it too personally though."

"Oh yeah? How would you take it?"

"Well, he went to see you on purpose. He knew you would be there."

"True," I say, considering her point. "But maybe he just wanted to see how bad of a mess I am."

"Oh please, if you're a mess than I'm a dumpster fire. No, he *wanted* to see you again."

I let myself entertain that for a moment. If he did want to see me, why would he behave so cold toward me?

As if Trisha can read my mind, she says, "I'm sure the only reason he wasn't exactly a chatty Cathy is because he didn't realize how seeing you again would make him feel."

It's my turn to laugh. "Yeah, you weren't there. It was chillier than the arctic circle."

A barista brings over Trisha's latte, and she sips through a devious smile.

"I guess we'll see."

Wanting desperately to change the subject, I blurt, "So you and Eddie Dearing, huh?"

Trisha erupts into giggles again. "I know, right?" she says. "He is just the most wonderful husband, though. I never saw it coming, myself. One day we got to talking at the hardware store, I was buying paint for my little rental at the time. One thing led to another, we started dating, and..." she trails off, seemingly enraptured by her memories. "The rest is history."

I think to myself how great it is that Eddie and Trisha can put the past behind them, knowing how Trisha helped bully Eddie in school. I must look deep in thought because Trisha does her mind reader thing again.

"I know what you're thinking," she says. "How can Eddie and I be so in love when I was so awful to him in high school?"

Busted. "I mean, I wasn't really..."

Trisha puts a hand up.

"I know that I was not a very kind person as a teenager. You don't have to beat around the bush. I apologized to Eddie for how my friends and I treated him, and we were able to move past it. I'm lucky that he's a very forgiving person." She smiles at me. "Time heals all wounds."

I think of Cam, and his ice-cold demeanor. *Not all wounds.*

"That brings me to my next point," Trisha says, her voice a little shaky. She clears her throat and looks me in the eye. I can see tears have begun to well up in her eyes. "Lizzie, I was not very nice to you, either. The things my group of friends and I did and said to you, well, they were inexcusable. *Especially...*" she trails off, and looks down at the table. She doesn't say it, but she doesn't have to. "Could you ever forgive me?"

I tilt my head, my mouth dropping open slightly. *Is she for real?*

"Trisha, of course. It's in the past, no harm no foul."

She reaches across the table and grabs my forearms, her eyes desperate.

"I mean it, Lizzie. Say you'll forgive me."

I swallow hard, a little alarmed by the sudden turn the conversation has taken.

"I forgive you, Trisha," I say to her, and she launches back in her chair, clapping her hands in front of her. She is back to her usual self.

"Oh, wonderful!" she exclaims. "I do hope we can be friends, Lizzie. For however long you're in town."

The earnestness in her voice catches me off guard, but warms me at the same time. That kind of candid sincerity isn't exactly abundant in Manhattan, especially coupled with the apology I just received. I wonder if I have grown so used to the disingenuous, kill-or-be-killed mentality of my job and the big city, that I've forgotten what it's like to prioritize friendships over the next big project, promotion, or prize trip to Bali. I look at Trisha, and smile.

"Me, too."

· · · ·

A FEW HOURS LATER, there is a tarp on the roof of Gran's house being held down by sandbags, and two younger guys are packing up a ladder onto a beat-up truck. I decide to head to Golden Acres to check on Gran and see how she's settling in, and tell her about the roof situation.

When I arrive at Gran's apartment, she is seated in the living room in front of the television. She does not look up when I enter, just sighs heavily. *Typical.*

"Hello, gran," I say, practically shouting over the ear-splitting volume of the game show she is watching. She grunts in response, then dials the volume up. I walk around the khaki-colored couch to face her, bending down to switch off the TV. Gran mumbles something unintelligible, but I assume it's something close *wretched girl.*

"Gran," I say, doing my best to keep my voice upbeat. "How long has the roof of the house been leaking?"

Scowling, Gran looks away and doesn't answer.

"It rained last night, and a lot of water got inside. I had someone come out and take a look at it, apparently it's pretty old and needs replacing."

This gets Gran's attention. She snaps her head toward me.

"The roof is fine! It doesn't need to be replaced, what a load of bologna!"

"Gran," I say, trying to reason with her. "I'm afraid it does. The roof is damaged enough that it's actually very dangerous."

She swats at me, as if to say I'm full of it, then crosses her arms over her chest. After a moment, she adds, "I suppose you're going to tell me you're selling the house, then? And this," she gestures to the small living room of her new apartment, "is where I can look forward to spending the remainder of my life?"

My throat tightens. "No one is selling anything, Gran. The house just can't sit in disrepair, is all." *A lie.* I sit down next to her and take her hand, ignoring how she flinches when I touch her. "Selling the house would be your decision. I just want to make sure it's ready in case you need to."

As the words come out of my mouth, I can't help but be sickened with myself. Eventually, there won't be a choice *but* to sell the house. Golden Acres Assisted Living might be affordable now, but if Gran's health and memory continue to decline, and they *will*, the cost of her care will increase dramatically. Gran knows this – she's heard it from me, from Cheryl, and her doctor – but she hasn't accepted it yet. If I know my Gran, she never will. By the time a decision needs to be made, it will be mine to make as her power of attorney, a thought that doesn't comfort me much. I look around her tiny new apartment, comfortable and efficient, and can see that it's not a home. It's a waystation, a temporary place. The thought chills me to the bone.

I squeeze Gran's hand lightly, overcome with a desire to comfort her that catches me completely off guard. My stomach roils as I think about the last ten years, and the fact that I haven't been around nearly as much as I probably should have been. If I had been, could we have caught Gran's dementia earlier on? The logical part of my brain tells me no, this is an unfortunate inevitability, and there is nothing I can do or could have done differently. I'm here now, and that's what matters.

That's what matters to you.

The devil that has been on my shoulder since the moment I arrived in Rocky Point whispers into my ear, saying the thing I've been avoiding since moving Gran into the facility. Am I here for Gran, really? Or am I here to stave off any further guilt I might feel for hightailing it out of town ten years ago, and never looking back?

I squeeze Gran's hand again, and this time, she looks at me. Her eyes grow wide as she takes in my face, that familiar twinkle twisting my stomach into knots. She smiles at me, reaches up with her other hand, and touches my cheek.

"Jeannine? Is that really you?"

The hairs on the back of my neck stand up and the sound of my mother's name.

Rocky Point, Massachusetts, August 2009

Slowly, carefully, I shut the front door of the house and turn the deadbolt, holding my breath so as not to make a sound. As soon as the deadbolt lock clicks shut, the lights in the foyer flick on and I jump, whirling around and pressing my back against the door.

Busted.

Gran stands at the foot of the stairs, clad in a blue cotton night-gown, arms folded over her chest. She is wearing the same scowl she always gives me, except this time, there is anger burning behind her eyes. I swallow hard, knowing I'm in big trouble, but trying my best to maintain my rebellious demeanor. I scowl back.

"What in God's name are you doing out so late, Elizabeth?" Gran snaps, and I shrug my shoulders in place of an answer. It's past midnight, and my curfew is 9PM. We both know I snuck out, so I don't see the point in saying it out loud.

Gran descends the last step and bridges the few feet between us, glaring at me. She sniffs at my clothes.

"So what was it, you went to a party? Were you drinking? Doing drugs? Out with it," she snaps, and I am appalled she would even think that of me.

"No way!" I shout back, pushing past Gran and stomping toward the kitchen. "I was out with Cam, we weren't doing anything like that."

In fact, Cam and I had been drinking milkshakes at the 24-hour diner in town. Afterward, we'd gone down to the harbor and watched for a comet that was supposed to be passing by. I don't tell Gran any of it, though, I'm too upset that she would even assume I'd been doing drugs of all things. Plus, I can tell she doesn't believe me.

"Oh sure, of course," she says. "Like I haven't heard that before."

"It's true!" I yell, pouring myself a glass of water.

"Sure it is, and I'm Mother Theresa. You know what? You're just like your mother."

I freeze, mid-gulp with my glass of water. I lower the glass slowly, biting back the tears stinging my eyes. Gran points a finger at me.

"You're exactly like her. She got into everything at your age, drinking and partying until all hours of the night, and what did that do for her? It got her pregnant, and addicted to drugs, that's what."

"Please stop," I say, my voice just barely above a whisper. "I wasn't doing anything like that, I swear."

"She swore all the time she wasn't doing it, and where is she now? On the streets somewhere getting high, maybe dead. Is that what you want?"

"No. I'm nothing like that," I plead, but Gran keeps on.

"And don't even get me started on your father. You want to end up in jail like him? Keep getting yourself into trouble."

"I'm nothing like either of them!" I shout, but Gran just crosses her arms again and shakes her head.

"I can't even look at you. Every time I do, all I see is your mother at your age," she makes a point of looking away from me, turning her head dramatically toward the wall, and pointing toward the stairs. "Go to your room. I don't need a constant reminder of how I failed as a mother hanging around."

Dropping my glass into the sink, I do as I'm told, holding back the lump in my throat until I'm behind my closed bedroom door. Only then, when she can't see me, do I allow myself to cry.

Chapter Five

Elizabeth

I LEAVE SHORTLY AFTER Cheryl arrives to keep Gran company, desperate to get out of there even though my conscience feels like it's weighing me down. By the time I pull up to Gran's house, I can feel that my face has become puffy and swollen from crying. When I spot the black pickup truck in the driveway, emblazoned on the side with *Tate Construction*, I do the best I can to wipe my face. Glancing in the rearview mirror, I can see I've only made it worse.

Oh, well.

Cameron exits his truck as I slide out of my car, adjusting the blue baseball cap on top of his head. He walks around to me, hands jammed into the pockets of his faded jeans, and stops with a few feet between us.

"Hi," I say, not really able to muster much more.

"I just wanted to stop by and make sure everything worked out alright with the roof," he says, skipping the pleasantries. He appears to look straight through me, which is fine with me since I look like I just spent a few hours in a small room slicing onions.

"Oh," I say, grinding my toe into the ground. "Yeah, thanks. They said it probably needs replacing."

"I know," he says, "Don't worry though, we'll take care of it for you. Have to order some materials, but should get them in a few days, a week at most. The tarp should hold you over until then."

"A few days to a week?" I rub my forehead and inhale a sharp breath. "Okay, not a problem."

"Got plans or something?" he asks, and I chuckle.

"Just, you know, work," I reply. "It's fine, though, I'll let them know I need some time off."

Cameron narrows his eyes at me.

"Are you alright?"

"Fine," I say, but we both know I don't mean it.

"Helen?" he asks, and I nod my head. Cam is no stranger to the many facets my mine and Gran's relationship, so not much more context is needed.

"I think I forgot for a moment that she can't stand the sight of me."

We stand in a tense, awkward silence for a few moments, and I want to kick myself for saying anything. I sound pathetic. *Pity party, party of one.*

To my surprise, Cam doesn't flee screaming from my pitiful self. Instead, he gives me a sympathetic smile.

"I'm sure it's tough, but you're doing the right thing," he says, his voice softening. "If I was in your shoes, I'd be making the same decision."

His words stun me, and I stand there with my mouth half open, wanting to say something to the contrary but not finding the words. I want to tell him to stop, to tell me how much of a terrible person I am. *Why is he defending me?* After everything I put him through when we were kids, shouldn't he be angry at me?

"You don't have to be nice to me," I say, the best I can do. He knits his brows together.

"What are you talking about?" he asks.

"You don't have to be nice," I repeat. "You of all people are allowed to tell me what a shit person I am for leaving and never looking back. For coming back after ten damn years for the sole purpose of putting my only relative into a nursing home so I don't have to deal with it."

He takes a step closer to me, and I instinctively take a step back.

"Elizabeth, your grandmother is sick. Nobody blames you for what you're doing."

"I blame me," I say, cursing myself for the tears welling up, threatening to spill over. I hate how vulnerable I'm allowing myself to be around him.

"Well, you've always been hardest on yourself."

I let his words sink in, taking a deep breath to try and collect my-self. Once I manage to corral my emotions, I stand up a little straighter.

"Thank you," I say. "And thank you for coming to check on the roof."

"Sure," he says. "Do you mind if I take a look at the ceiling inside again? I just want to see how it looks now that it's dry."

"Oh, of course," I say. "Come on in."

He follows me into the house, heading upstairs to look at the ceil-ing while I sit down at the kitchen table, in front of a box of Gran's im-portant personal documents. Cheryl suggested I contact Gran's lawyer to discuss her will and wishes, a conversation I am so *not* looking for-ward to, and I need to locate the most recent copy of her will. I'm still staring at the box, lid still on and everything, when Cam returns down-stairs.

"Well, we're definitely going to need to do some work on that ceil-ing. I hate to say it, but it's rotting through."

Great. I squeeze my eyes tightly shut, praying that I don't lose it. "Will that take long to fix?"

"Hard to say." Cam sits down at the kitchen table next to me, re-moving his baseball cap and running a hand through his hair. "We'll need to replace the exterior roof first, to prevent any further damage. Once that's done, we'll have to evaluate the extent of the rot on the in-side and the make any necessary repairs. Could take anywhere from a few extra days, to a few weeks, depending on the damage."

The news is like a sucker punch to the gut. I can't see how I would be able to take multiple weeks off work without risking my job alto-gether, but the uncertainty surrounding gran's condition doesn't leave me many options.

"I'll figure it out and let you know," I say, my throat suddenly dry. I stand up from the table abruptly and root around in the cabinets for a glass. "Water?" I ask Cam, the panic evident in my voice.

"No, thank you."

Breathe, I tell myself, feeling a panic attack brewing. Finally finding a glass, I turn on the faucet and freeze when a loud banging noise echoes throughout the house.

"What the..."

It sounds like someone is banging pots and pans together from inside the wall. The floor shakes a little every time the sound reverberates, and no water comes out of the faucet.

Cam jumps up from his chair.

"Turn it off!" he shouts, and I do as I'm told, setting the glass down and slowly backing away from the sink.

"What was that?" I ask, and I can hear Cam gulp audibly.

"Whatever it was, it's probably not good," he says, pulling out his cell phone. "I have a friend who's a plumber, I'll have him come over and take a look."

I nod, officially out of words to verbalize how badly I want to wake up from the nightmare I'm currently living in. Cam must be able to sense that I'm on the verge of a meltdown because he doesn't say anything, just clears his throat and looks at the floor.

"There is no way I'm going to be able to sell this house," I groan, massaging my temples and inhaling a deep breath.

"You're planning to sell it?" Cam asks, and something in his voice has the hair on the back of my neck standing at attention.

"Well, yeah eventually," I say. "Gran is going to be in the nursing home pretty permanently, and my life is back in New York, so..."

I let my voice trail off, feeling like I've inadvertently ripped open an old wound. Cameron's eyes are dark, and I can't quite read what's behind them. His mouth drawn into a tight line, he jams his hands in his pockets once again.

"Right, that makes sense," he says. "I don't know, I just thought you might be in town for a while."

His deep blue gaze locks onto mine, and goosebumps explode over my skin, sending a long-forgotten chill down my spine. It's the way he's looking at me, the tension in his jaw and the rigidness of his stance while his eyes are screaming to me, that causes my heart to practically gallop out of my chest. I feel my lips part slightly, my body both wanting to move and not daring to at the same time, for fear that the electricity around us might strike me down at any moment.

He rakes his eyes over me, taking his time as they move from my face down my body and back up, hesitating a moment before looking back into my eyes. I feel like I want to explode into a million pieces, and my brain is on fire, dying to know what he's thinking. My cheeks burn as I wonder, *does he like what he sees? Or does he think he dodged a bullet all those years ago?* My breath hitches in my throat when I realize that I really, desperately hope it's not the latter.

"I... um...." The words stumble out of my mouth, and Cameron smirks.

"I should be going," he says, grabbing his baseball cap off the table and returning it to his head. "I'll send someone out to take a look at that sink. Let me know what you decide about the roof." I nod, and trail behind him as he heads to the front door. He opens it, but turns to me before he leaves. "If you still wanted to catch up sometime, let me know. You know where to find me."

Before I can pick my jaw up off the floor, he is out the door and in his truck, backing out of the driveway. A smile tugs at the corner of my mouth, one thought crossing my mind:

I guess I know what he was thinking.

Chapter Six

Cameron

MOST PEOPLE DESPISE Mondays, but for most of my adult life, I've enjoyed them. Monday mornings always feel like a fresh start. A clean slate. Most days I wake up with the sun, so I always make it a point to take a few minutes first thing on Monday morning, sip my coffee, and soak in the beauty of a new day, a fresh start.

This Monday, though, just started off wrong. I felt distracted, on edge, like things had been thrown slightly off balance. I knew why, of course. I'd gone ahead and opened Pandora's box, and let Lizzie get back under my skin. My plan had been to stay away, but the minute I saw her in her driveway Sunday night, her eyes puffy and swollen, her cheeks still wet from fresh tears, I couldn't help myself. I felt an instinctual, almost animalistic need to protect her, to make her okay. I'd known right away the issue was Helen. The issue was *always* Helen. I felt awful telling her how long the roof would take to fix, and I couldn't anticipate the plumbing breaking, but as the issues piled up and I could see the stress wearing her down, I didn't know what else to do. I just knew I needed to make it better. And the best way I could think to do that was to offer to be there for her. I had put the ball in her court, though. I didn't want to come off too strong, but I also wanted to see how she'd react, if she'd reach out.

I'd gone to work like a zombie on Monday morning, drifting through the day like a dinghy out in rough, open seas, letting the waves and the current take me wherever they saw fit. I went with the flow, half of me in the present and half of me stuck inside my own head, on thought playing over and over again:

Is she going to call me?

It's pathetic, I know. But as much as I hate to admit it, my mom's and Eddie's words had started to get under my skin. All that bullshit about a second chance, about the universe tossing it right in my lap, had made me actually start to wonder if that were true. The problem, though, is that Lizzie isn't planning to stick around. She's fixing up her grandmother's house, listing it for sale, and then getting the hell out of Rocky Point and going back to her life in New York City. She'd told me as much. What am I supposed to do, convince her to leave her entire life behind and come back to Rocky Point for good? Not likely. And if I put my heart on the line again, and she leaves, *again?* Would I be able to come back from that? I'm not sure.

When I still haven't heard from her on Wednesday, I'm in a right foul mood. My employees are avoiding me, communicating everything through Hank, one of my Foremen, and ducking out of my way whenever they see me. I don't blame them; I've snapped at some pretty trivial shit the last few days. I snapped at Eddie Dearing, too, when he told me a shipment of supplies I ordered from him was running late. I know it's a risk I take ordering only from small local businesses, but damn if wasn't pissed to have to push back the timetable on a couple of projects, including Lizzie's grandmother's house.

Considering that the delayed timeframe I gave Lizzie was already too long for her liking, I seriously doubt she's going to appreciate that we might be looking at tacking on an additional week. After moping around my office for a few hours avoiding having to deliver the news, I suck it up, get in my truck, and drive over to Helen's house, hoping that I can put my hurt pride aside for a while and keep *the* conversation strictly business.

Not likely.

When I pull up to Helen's house, I notice that the shiny black Lexus that Lizzie had been driving is nowhere to be found. Instead, there's a little silver SUV in the driveway, the hatch open in the back to reveal a trunk full of stacked boxes labeled by room. I park my truck next to the SUV, watching as an older, portly woman in pink scrubs ambles out of Helen's front door, her plump arms wrapped around two more large boxes.

I hop out of the truck and jog up to her, relieving her of the boxes and earning a grateful smile.

"Why thank you, dear! That's truly kind of you," the woman says, opening one of the SUV's doors so I can slide the boxes into the back seat. "I'm married, though, so I hope you don't have any ulterior motives."

I laugh, gripping the back of my neck.

"Actually, I'm looking for Elizabeth Quinn," I say, shaking the woman's hand. "I'm Cameron Tate. My company, Tate Construction, is working on the roof."

"Ah, well," the woman says, looking me up and down. I shift on my feet, uncomfortable. "A girl can dream. I'm Cheryl, Ms. Helen's personal caregiver."

"Nice to meet you."

She closes the doors and the hatch on the trunk, then turns to face me.

"I'm sorry, but Elizabeth isn't here," she explains, shrugging her shoulders and smiling sympathetically. "She went back to New York on Sunday evening. Is there a message I can give her?"

It takes a second for Cheryl's words to sink in. I grind my back teeth together, the tension in my jaw sending a twinge of pain up my cheek. "She left on Sunday? Did she say when she'd be back?" I ask, the words coming out as more of a growl then I intended. Cheryl knits her brows together.

"No," she says, her confusion obvious. "I'm not sure when she'll back, but I can pass along a message if you'd like. Is something the matter with the roof?"

I shake my head. "No, I just wanted to give her an update on some materials I ordered. It can wait."

My life is back in New York, she had told me. Clearly.

Cheryl climbs into the driver's side of her SUV and waves as she backs out, leaving me standing like an idiot alone in Helen's driveway.

When I hadn't heard from Lizzie, I'd assumed she just didn't want to get any closer than our recent professional relationship. I hadn't anticipated that she would just up and leave so quickly. I thought that, maybe, she shared the spark I felt, too. Oh well, I have my answer and that's all I need to know. When... *if...* she comes back to Rocky Point, I'll make sure the roof and plumbing get taken care of, and that's it. No catching up. No second chances.

I climb back into my car and see that my cell phone is blinking. Unlocking the screen, I scroll through several text messages and missed calls from my mother:

Missed Call: *Mom*

Mom: *Cameron, your brother will be the death of me.*

Mom: *Cameron, have you seen the tabloids?*

Missed Call: *Mom*

Missed Call: *Mom*

Mom: *It said something about "spilling the tea" on his new girlfriend. Why would he spill tea on someone? Did you know he had a girlfriend?*

Mom: *What does "on fleek" mean?*

Missed Call: *Mom*

Mom: *Did he tell you he had a girlfriend?*

I roll my eyes and dial her back, preparing my speech about not paying attention to the tabloids. My brother Grayson, an aspiring actor, has recently landed himself a recurring role on a popular Soap Opera. Mom and I had this talk once before, when I found her glued to her computer screen, Googling Grayson's name and scrolling endlessly through random corners of the internet looking for gossip about him, proof that he's "made it." I didn't think we'd have to have it again so soon, but here we are.

She picks up on the first ring, like she has been eagerly anticipating my call. I can practically hear her vibrating on the other end of the line, unable to contain herself.

"Well, did you see it?" she asks.

I respond with a long, drawn-out sigh, and then, "No. I did not see it."

"Oh, Cameron it's awful. Apparently he spilled tea all over his girl-friend on their first date," she says. "I think. I didn't know Grayson drank tea, to be honest."

"Mom, 'spilling the tea' doesn't mean spilling *actual* tea. It Gen Z speak for gossiping," I explain. There is a long beat of silence on the other end while mom contemplates my lesson in today's hip slang.

"Hmm," she finally says. "Well, that's better than literally spilling tea, I suppose. Now, what about that other word?"

"Which word?"

"*Fleek.*"

"It means to look good."

"Now that's just silly."

"Are you going to tell me what this is about?" I ask impatiently.

"Your brother's new girlfriend!" she says. "He just got a part on that Soap Opera, what's it called? *While the Globe Spins?* Anyway, suppos-edly he's dating his co-star, who plays his love interest on the show!"

That piques my curiosity, since I'm pretty sure that most of the ac-tresses in that show are *super* famous. I put the call on speaker phone while I look it up. Sure enough, the first headline from The Daily Star, a popular tabloid magazine, proclaims: *Grayson Tate, TV's Newest Heartthrob, Snags a New Beau. Could There Be Trouble Brewing? Tea Will Be Spilled.*

I have to do a double take, because the picture associated with the article is of Grayson in jeans, a t-shirt, and sunglasses holding hands with a very familiar-looking woman. She's tall and leggy, with bronzed skin and jet-black hair that cascades in a pin-straight curtain down her back and over her shoulders. She's wearing sunglasses too, but she is un-mistakable. It's Ariana Lopez, famed actress and singer, and Grayson's co-star on the show.

Holy shit. "I didn't see that coming."

"I'm concerned," my mom says. "These types of things never end well. I think you should call him and tell him to knock it off."

"Oh, come on," I say. "He's out in L.A. with a legit acting gig, dating a super-hot, famous actress. He's living the dream."

"He's going to get hurt. He should just be focusing on his career, not getting distracted by some drama queen actress."

"Mom, you have to let Gray make his own decisions. This is what he wanted."

"Fine, but can you at least call him? Just to check in."

"Fine."

"Have I ever told you you're my favorite son?"

Chapter Seven

Elizabeth

THURSDAY MORNING, I am in the car bright and early, headed back up to Rocky Point and finding the long drive up the New England coast strangely cathartic this time around. Almost the minute I cross over the NYC border, I feel the stress melt away and realize I can't wait to take in the scenery and have some time to breathe. Between Gran's health and the state of her house, it's clear I'm needed in Rocky Point pretty badly. Unfortunately, I just hadn't planned on how *long* I'd be needed.

I checked out of my hotel Sunday night and left Rocky Point, heading back to NYC, work, and my normal life for a few days. Leaving Rocky Point felt wrong, but I hadn't cleared time off beyond the weekend with my boss, and I knew she wouldn't react very well if I called out. I hadn't expected Gran to be so bad, though, and the farther and farther I got from Rocky Point, the guiltier I felt. Cheryl had promised to keep an eye on Gran so that I could tie up a few loose ends on my current work projects, and work out some extended time off. I have a ton of unused vacation time, plus some holiday comp time I can take, which easily gives me a few weeks off if I need it. My boss wasn't thrilled when I told her – actually, that's an understatement. Whitney was thoroughly pissed, and didn't hesitate to tell me how much of a lurch I was leaving her in. Thankfully, she didn't threaten to fire me, which I half expected. I do, however, fully expect her to make my life a living hell upon my return. *Oh, well.* I'll deal with that after I deal with everything else.

There is a ton to be done if the goal is to get Gran's house ready to sell, and make sure her affairs are in order. I need to make sure whatever work needs done on the house gets taken care of, and to schedule a meeting with Gran's lawyer to discuss her situation. With any luck, the damage to the roof and drywall won't be nearly as bad as it seems.

I won't know for sure, though, until Cam and his crew can get started, which is why my first stop when I get back into town is Tate Construction.

The thought twists my stomach into a knot.

As much as I loathe to admit it, I haven't been able to stop thinking about Cam since I left town on Sunday. What started as a few morbidly curious thoughts weaseling their way into my long drive home soon turned in to a full-blown preoccupation, and now I'm lucky if I go ten minutes without finding myself drifting off into daydream-land. It's not even that he's got some ruggedly adorable *thing* going on that makes my insides turn to jelly. Ever since we first ran into each other, the night Trisha sent him charging through the rain to my rescue, it's just felt like we have ... *unfinished business.* I keep replaying the way he looked at me, like I was a giant ugly blobfish one minute, and then something he wanted to devour the next. How's a girl supposed to just *not* think about that?

I pull into the gravel parking lot of Tate Construction's headquarters, a small office building on the inland side of town that is home to largely blue collar businesses – a machine shop, an auto auction and scrap yard, and a small trucking company, to name a few. Tate Construction sits on a large lot, with a modern, inviting office building positioned close to the street, and a large warehouse occupying the back half. I look around in awe at the place, trying to wrap my head around Cam building it from the ground up. He'd always wanted to make his own way – by the looks of things, he'd done just that.

Stepping inside the office building, I'm greeted by a young redhead at the front desk. She flashes me a warm smile when she sees me, her teeth perfectly straight and a bright, brilliant white. She stands to greet me, revealing a tall, slender figure and hair that cascades in waves down her back. Her large, emerald eyes are rimmed with thick, dark lashes, and I have to admit, I'm actually a little frightened by how pretty she is. *Is Cam hiring models to work for him or something?* She reaches out her hand to shake mine, and I respond in kind, feeling a little self-conscious about how... *delicate* her hand feels.

"Hello, ma'am, my name is Kylie. How can I help you?"

Ma'am? I figure she can't be more than 21, but still! I'm not that old.

"Hi, Kylie," I say, more curtly than I intended, but oh well. "I'm here to see Cam, if he's available?"

She cocks her head to the side, her strawberry waves fluttering over her shoulder. "I'm sorry?"

For some ungodly reason, I can feel myself beginning to sweat. Kylie is looking at me like I'm an alien with ten heads, and I can't help but take it personally. *Why does Cam need a secretary that looks like she could be strutting the runway in stilettos and angel wings?*

"Cam," I repeat, "is he here?"

"Sorry, ma'am, I'm not sure who you mean."

I blink a few times, and then try, "I'm here to see Mr. Tate."

"*Oh,* Mr. Tate," Kylie says, as if I'd suddenly just started speaking a language she can understand. "Please take a seat, I'll let him know you're here."

Kylie floats around to the other side of the desk and gestures to a plush leather chair, then glides lithely down a hallway and around a corner. I opt to stand, my nerves getting the better of me and my attitude still a little bent from the runway model receptionist. *Why am I so nervous to see him?* My stomach twists into knots as I think about the last conversation we had. *He wants to catch up.* Is that a good idea? I don't have enough time to debate that with myself, however, because it's only a moment before Kylie is strutting back down the hallway, leading Cam right into the reception area.

Cam clashes with the modern, professional décor of the office in his faded jeans and flannel shirt. His face, which was clean shaven a few days ago, is now scruffy and unkempt. In high school, Cam was a boy-next-door, prom king sort of cute, and years of football had given him an athletic build. This older, grown up version of Cam feels much more *bad boy*, deliciously rumpled with well-built muscles and a gaze with years more experience behind it. A gaze that makes me squirm when it meets my own.

His eyes widen at the sight of me, just for a split second, before narrowing into a scowl. I smile awkwardly, but he doesn't return the gesture. I let out a long sigh. *Guess we're back to blobfish.*

"Your visitor, Mr. Tate. A Mrs....?"

Kylie looks at me, and I don't even care, I roll my eyes in plain sight of her.

"*Miss* Quinn," I say. "Elizabeth Quinn." Not that it matters or anything, I'm just still riled over the whole *ma'am* business.

"Right," she says. "Please let me know if there's anything else you need."

I glower at her as she sashays behind the desk, then turn back to Cam, who is still scowling at me. There's a tension in the air so dense, I can practically taste it.

"I didn't expect to see you," he says, crossing his arms over his chest. "I stopped by Helen's on Monday, but you were gone."

"Yes," I reply, wringing my hands in front of me. I hadn't explicitly said I was going back to New York for a few days. Is that why he's looking at me like a bad hairball? "I had some loose ends to tie up with work."

"Hmm," he grumbles, nodding his head. "I thought maybe you just left. Wouldn't be the first time."

I can feel my cheeks burning. "I had to work out some time off, to take care of the house and all."

He tilts his head to the side, staring silently at me for a moment before the slightest smirk tugs at the corner of his mouth, causing my stomach to flutter.

"So, you're planning to stick around?"

"For a little while," I say, and try not to melt when a full-blown smile spreads across his face. I can feel my palms beginning to sweat. *Get a grip, girl.* "And I could really use some help with that roof, if your team is still available."

"I think we can find some time."

My throat feels like a desert. "Great," I say, steeling my nerves. "And as a thank you, I really would love to buy you a drink sometime." Cam cocks his eyebrow, and I add, "if you still wanted to catch up, that is."

His eyes twinkle mischievously. "I think I can find some time." I gulp audibly, and he adds, "Ryan's? Say around seven?"

Ryan's Pub is a small, low key bar and restaurant in town with a nice view of the water. It's usually less crowded than some of the more traditional bars, at least from what I remember.

"I'll be there," I say.

"Looking forward to it." He says it with palpable intent that sends a shiver of anticipation through me.

Yes, I think to myself, *this is an awfully bad idea.*

Chapter Eight

I DUCK INTO MY OFFICE and close the door behind me, pulling out my cell phone and dialing Grayson's phone number. Mom wanted me to check up on him, but I think I need his advice more than he needs mine right now. Some big brother I am. At the end of the day, though, he's the one dating the hot actress and I'm the one getting all tangled up by the girl who broke my heart.

It rings a few times, then goes to voicemail.

Shit.

I dial him again, growing impatient as it rings a few times. Finally, just as I think it's about to go to voicemail again, a grumpy, groggy-sounding Grayson picks up on the other end.

"What do you want?"

"Wow, Gray, it's great to talk to you, too."

"It's Goddamn nine in the morning here, in case you forgot there's a three-hour time difference between Rocky Point and L.A." he grumbles.

"Oh, I'm sorry. Us people with real jobs are usually up before nine on a weekday. Sorry to disturb your beauty sleep."

"Shut up, I have a real job," Grayson whines. "Now what do you want?"

"I... uh..."

"Spit it out, Cam."

"Lizzie is back in town."

A heavy silence hangs on Gray's end of the line, and I wait, letting him react. When everything blew up between Lizzie and I, Gray had been a freshman in high school. She'd been such a big part of my life up until that point, such a big part of our family, that for Gray, it had been like losing a big sister. He'd taken it pretty hard, too.

His sullen voice finally croaks out a response on the other end of the line. "For good?"

"No," I say. "Just while she gets her grandmother's affairs in order. Helen Quinn was recently diagnosed with dementia, and Lizzie had to move her into a nursing home. She's getting the house ready to sell, but there have been a lot of... well, it needs a lot of work."

I'm met with another lengthy silence.

"Cam, don't tell me you're doing the repairs," Grayson says, his tone stern but also warped with concern. I let out a long sigh, confirming for him what he probably already figured. "Jesus, Cam, are you some kind of masochist or something?"

"No, come on. It's not like that," I say, but I know as well as he does that it's absolute, 100% bullshit.

"Right, you just happened to be the only handyman available? Look Cam, I don't mean to be an asshole, but she ditched you like it was nothing. She didn't even tell you she was going away to college until right before she left. She broke your heart, man."

"Thanks Gray, I think I remember," I say through gritted teeth. Why did I think it would be a good idea to run this by him, again?

"Okay, so what? You're just going to let her use you until she leaves again?" he says. "If she's selling the house, she *is* leaving again."

For some reason, this makes me angry. She's not using me, I offered to help. And I'm well aware that she's going to leave again. She told me as much. But for some unknown reason, I can't help but feel weirdly protective over her. Besides, it's not like Gray knew the whole story of how we broke up, not really. He only knew the parts that angry, depressed me wanted to tell at the time. I know she didn't *want* to break up. I'd just made it seem like it was her only option.

"It's not like that. And honestly Gray, you were too young to get it back then. I basically told her to pick between me and college. If anything, *I* was the asshole," I say. Even though he is silent, I can tell he's contemplating what I've said.

"That's one way to spin it, I guess," he grunts.

"Mom thinks I should try to win her back," I tell him, and he snorts a laugh.

"Of course she does. Mom watches way too many Hallmark movies."

"Well, I'm meeting up with Lizzie tonight. At Ryan's."

"Look man, just be careful. I get it, you need some kind of closure or whatever. Just don't think she won't break your heart this time. She did it once, she'll do it again."

"I know."

"And maybe she'll surprise you, who knows," Gray adds in a slightly more upbeat tone.

"Maybe."

"Not trying to be a Debbie-downer, Cam. Just looking out for my big brother, is all."

"Thanks, Gray," I say. "Really, I appreciate it. I think that's why I called, I just needed someone to give me a little dose of reality before I do this."

"Anytime."

"So, about that actress you're dating," I say, switching the subject because I've had about as much heartbreak talk as I can take for today.

"Oh man, is mom reading the tabloids again?" Gray asks, laughing.

"She is. Ariana Lopez? Really?"

"It's not that serious," Gray insists. "We're coworkers. We just like to hang out and have some fun outside of work together, that's it."

Typical Grayson. Before he left for L.A., he had a bit of a reputation around town for being a ladies' man. He'd dated a different girl practically every week in high school. When he got older, he'd made it a habit of trying to pick up tourists at some of the trendier bars in town, especially during the summer season when local hotels were booked solid. It was the same story with every woman he met – *it's not that serious.* But somehow, those little flings still always ended with a slap across the face or a drink being dumped on his head. I have a feeling this isn't too different.

"Dating coworkers can be tricky," I say.

"Come on, Cam. Can you blame me?"

Admittedly, I can't.

"Wasn't she in the swimsuit edition of Sports Illustrated last year?" I ask.

"Yeah. Pretty cool, huh?"

"I think it might be my turn to give you a lecture," I say.

"No, honestly, it's not anything serious. The tabloids are always going to make it seem like more than it is."

"You were holding hands, Gray. Does she know it's not that serious?"

"I'm not having this conversation right now! Tell mom to *stop* reading those garbage magazines. You too," he says.

"Fine," I say. "But you better bring her home for Thanksgiving. I want my copy of Sports Illustrated autographed."

"You're an idiot," he says. He can't see me, but I nod my head. "Probably."

• • • •

ROCKY POINT, MASSACHUSETTS, July 2010
10 years earlier

"Dude, why are you being such an asshole lately?"

I turn on Grayson, who has been walking a few steps behind me the whole way home from getting ice cream at Cups and Cones, a local ice cream parlor in town and a Rocky Point staple. Their signature flavor, Rocky Point Road, is my favorite and I thought stuffing my face might cheer me up. It isn't helping, but neither is my annoying younger brother who keeps calling me an asshole.

"I don't know, Gray, maybe because my girlfriend dumped me and now I'm stuck hanging out with my loser brother."

"Are you sure you're not the loser? You're the one that got dumped."

I throw a glare over my shoulder at him and stuff my hands in my pockets. As much as it annoys me, he's not *wrong*. I feel like a loser.

It's only been a few weeks since Lizzie left for school, *and* left me behind, but I guess I just thought it wouldn't hurt as bad by now. I guess I thought that when she was gone, like *really* gone, it would somehow be easier to move on from. Out of sight, out of mind, right?

Not so much.

"I don't get why you're so upset, anyway," Gray continues, his long legs and lanky frame suddenly appearing next to me. "You're a free man. You can date any girl you want."

Typical Gray. Ever since starting high school, Gray has developed a bit of a reputation as a lady killer. I really can't understand why. His long, skinny legs make him look more like an antelope or some shit than a dude, but I guess that's what girls are into these days. I guess it probably doesn't hurt, either, that he's already on the varsity track team, despite just finishing his Freshman year.

"I don't *want* to date any girl," I say, keeping my eyes focused on the road in front of us and not on the pitying look Gray is sending me. "I want Lizzie. You couldn't possibly understand."

"You're right, I don't understand. Seems stupid to waste all this time wanting a girl you can't have," Gray scoffs, causing me to stop walking and roll my eyes, sighing loudly.

"I was going to marry her, dude. I wanted to ask her after graduation."

Gray stops walking too, turning to look at me with wide, surprised eyes. "Are you for real?"

"Yeah, man. I even looked at rings, but hadn't bought one yet because I was still saving up the money. And then..."

"And then she dumped your ass."

I narrow my eyes at him. "Yeah. And then she dumped my ass."

We continue walking in silence, Gray finally shutting up long enough to let me fester in my gross feelings. I had yet to reduce my breakup with Lizzie down to such terms, but in reality, it's the truth. Lizzie dumped my ass. And for some reason, I would do anything to have her back.

"I just wish I could turn back time and convince her not to go," I say.

"Why don't you just call her? You have her phone number, right?" Gray asks, condescension dripping from his voice.

"I can't, it's over. She won't talk to me, and she made it really clear she doesn't want anything to do with me anymore."

Gray claps me on the shoulder. "I'm sorry, man."

I shrug away from the gesture, turning up the driveway toward our house. There's no use in being sorry. I can't change anything, despite how much I'd like to. Lizzie is never coming back, and the sooner I get used to it, the better off I'll be.

Chapter Nine

Elizabeth

I SHOW UP TO RYAN'S about twenty minutes early, hoping to down at least one cocktail before Cam arrives for some liquid courage. I find a seat at the shiny mahogany bar, and quickly take stock of the room and other patrons. There's a couple all the way down at the other end of the bar, sitting close to each other and talking quietly. A group of four younger guys are sitting at a nearby table, talking and drinking beers, checking out another table of girls giggling over fruity mixed drinks and a plate of nachos. There are a few other guys in the back of the bar, shooting pool and talking smack. I'm grateful for the low-key atmosphere, because I can chug the vodka soda the bartender sets down in front of me without drawing too much attention. I hold up a hand to signal for another one, and within seconds, it appears in front of me.

I feel Cam enter the bar before I see him. Maybe it's the alcohol I've just shocked my system with, or some weird spidey-sense, but the hair on the back of my neck stands on end and I can feel his eyes zero in on me. I quickly gulp down my second drink and inhale a sharp breath.

Be...cool...

"Hope you weren't waiting too long," Cam says, his deep voice rumbling in my ear as he slides onto a chair next to me. The bartender comes over to us and Cam orders bourbon, then eyes my empty glass. "And another for the lady."

The bartender, an older woman with long silver hair and big, wide-set blue eyes, gives me a sideways glance, as if to remind me that this is my third drink in twenty minutes. I smile sheepishly at her, and she shakes her head as she walks away. *Traitor.*

"So, this is weird, huh?" Cam asks, causing me to laugh. I can feel the tension leave my shoulders as I relax a little.

"Very."

"You know, when Trisha called me the other day... the last thing I expected to hear was that you were back in town," he says, lowering his voice slightly as the bartender comes back with his bourbon.

"Trust me, I didn't expect to be back," I say, wanting to take it back as soon as the words leave my mouth.

"Life in the big city everything you hoped it would be?" He asks, turning to face me. He takes a swig of his bourbon, his eyes never leaving mine.

"Well..." I start, thinking of all the good things about my life in New York. My condo is nice, and in a pretty good area in Greenwich Village. I have a great job with even better benefits. I try to think up all the other perks, but am coming up embarrassingly empty. The silence drags on, and the bartender walks over with my drink in the meantime.

"Wow," he says, shaking his head. "I must admit, that sounds enthralling." The sarcasm drips from every word, and I can't say I blame him. I've done a pretty terrible job at justifying my choices.

"It's great," I say, ignoring the way he narrows his eyes at me.

"You know what you've never been very good at?" He asks, and I shrug my shoulders.

"What?"

"Lying."

I roll my eyes, but he and I both know he's got me there.

"Ok, well, it is great," I say. "New York is a fantastic city. Sure, my job gets stressful and competitive, but I love the work."

"What do you do, again?" he asks.

"I work for an ad agency. Think *Mad Men*, but with Keurigs and a lot more feminism."

"Right," he says, taking another sip of his bourbon. "Sounds fancy."

"Not as fancy as owning my own company," I shoot back, taking a long sip of my own drink from my straw. "Your offices are pretty impressive. Plus, you hire *models* to work for you."

"I'm sure I have no idea what you mean."

"Come *on*," I say. "The redhead at your front desk looks like she should be on the cover of Vogue."

"Oh, Kylie?" he asks, acting as if a lightbulb has just gone off in his head. "She's just a college kid who works for us part time. Why, you jealous?"

I roll my eyes again. "Not even close."

We chat for a while, my walls dropping the more he tells me about life since we last left off. I hear all about how Cam and his dad started Tate Construction together, just a few years after graduating high school, and turned it into a small but profitable business. How the most scared he'd ever been in his life was when his dad died suddenly of a heart attack the following year, leaving him as the sole owner of the business. What did a 21-year-old, barely of legal drinking age even and with no college degree, know about running and maintaining a business? He tells me how he almost gave up, until his mom convinced him he could do it, and that his dad would be so proud of him just for trying. He made a commitment then and there to devote all of his energy to making the business successful, working from sun-up to sun-down every day for two straight years until he was able to purchase that site and build the warehouse and offices.

I tell him about college, about working as much as I could to save up and put toward my tuition, being an R.A. for a break with room and board, and studying every minute I wasn't working or in class. I don't hold back when I tell him about winning a competitive and coveted internship with an ad agency on Fifth Avenue, where I went on to land a full time job immediately after graduation as an assistant to the Creative Director, eventually working my way up to director-level myself. I find it easy to be honest, and tell him the negatives, too. Like how my friends and coworkers would inevitably end up being my biggest competition, leading to many superficial friendships that didn't last very long. Or how romantic relationships are nearly impossible when you're working 14-hour days, so dating would be hit or miss and generally not get past a few dates before things fizzled out. He seems surprised at that last bit, which makes me laugh.

"I know you probably thought the high-stress atmosphere of my job and the city would make settling down easy," I joke, "but I assure you, it takes at least three dates to be sure the guy isn't a serial killer, and even that has some margin for error."

"And here I thought it was the small-town vibe killing my chances," Cam laughs.

By this point, the bartender has brought us two more rounds of drinks, and is making eyes at me like she's sizing up when to cut me off. Little does she know, my limit is usually three.

"So, no one serious in your life then?" I ask.

"There've been a few here and there, nothing that's lasted very long," he says. "Not unlike you, I've been a little married to my job the last few years. Doesn't exactly make it easy."

"When the time is right," I say.

"Exactly."

We lock eyes, as if the weight of our history is suddenly laid out on the bar in front of us. For some reason, I feel exactly like I did that day at the coffee shop, and want to reach my hand out across the short few inches of the bar top to take his. As if reading my mind, he lets go of his bourbon glass, his fingers twitching, as if daring me to. I look from him, to his hand, back to him, and watch his eyes go wide as saucers.

Should I say something first? I wonder. *Or just go for it?* I ready my hand for the possibility, the electricity in the air hanging between us like a curtain made of lightening.

"Lizzie, I..." Cam stutters, gulping audibly. His eyes widen even further, and I wonder if he's just as nervous as I am.

"What?" I ask, but he doesn't answer right away. He's starting to look... panicked? A bead of sweat is making its way from his hairline down the side of his face, which is now pale as a starched white sheet. *Oh boy,* I think to myself. *What have I done?* "Cam, what is it?"

I hear the disturbance in the force before I see it.

"Cameron Tate, you absolute *dog* of a man."

The hair on the back of my neck stands on end as I watch a tall, slender brunette stride past me, wearing a flowy sunflower-yellow dress cinched with a thin, brown belt. Her hands on her hips, she shimmies in between Cam and I as if she doesn't even know I'm there.

"I should've known you were a lying prick when you told me you needed to *work on yourself*," the woman shrieks, paying no mind to the silence that has settled over the bar or the eyes that are now suddenly on the three of us. She points a shiny, red manicured nail in my direction, but still does not actually acknowledge me. "Let me guess, *she's* helping you work on yourself?"

Something in the high-pitched tone of her voice, the way she stresses every third or fourth word, flashes me back to hiding in the girls' bathroom in seventh grade. Heat pricks at my skin, and I feel myself beginning to get flushed. *Oh God,* I think. *No. No, no, no...*

"Ainsley, look, could you maybe..." Cam starts, but he is cut off.

"Could I what? Lower my voice so the whole bar doesn't have to hear? Too late."

Ainsley Wells' voice is dripping with vitriol, but I'm too stunned to move, let alone feel any sort of offense at Ainsley's words. I can feel all of the bars' eyes on us, but all I can do is stare at the back of Ainsley's yellow dress, my brain trying to make sense of the events unfolding in front of me.

Ainsley's continues her tirade, hands flailing dramatically, and Cam's apologetic eyes drift past her to me. Seeing his attention divert, Ainsley whips around to shoot a fiery look in my direction. When her eyes meet mine, however, and after a moment of studying my face, Ainsley's eyes grow wide with recognition. She looks from Cam, to me, and then turns back to Cam, her mouth dropping open.

"Oh, you have *got* to be kidding me." Ainsley looks as though she might burst into flames. If looks could kill, Cam and I would be goners.

"*Her?*" The word, or maybe the way she says the word, cuts me like a knife. "Break up with me, and go running back to your high school girlfriend?"

"Break up with you?" I'm surprised when my voice breaks through Ainsley's rant, a quiet, mousey squeak. Cam's face has drained of all color, and the surprise I felt has now been replaced by a wave of embarrassment crashing over me. *I'm such a fool.*

"Yes," Ainsley hisses, turning her venom toward me. "I guess Cameron forgot to mention it to you."

I stand up abruptly, Ainsley's eyes bearing intently into me. Cam looks as though he might hurl, or bolt. I grab my jacket off the back of the chair, take a twenty out of my wallet, and slide it onto the bar.

"Seems like you two have some things to work out," I say. "I'm going to head out. Cam, it was nice catching up."

Ainsley scoffs and rolls her eyes, but Cam gets up from his chair. "Lizzie, wait a second!"

I don't wait, as I'd rather burn my eyes out with a hot poker than spend any more time in the presence of Ainsley Wells, and instead turn and walk calmly toward the door to the bar, despite wanting to run as fast as my legs can carry me. I hear heavy footsteps behind me, but press on out of the bar and through the parking lot until I'm standing at my car. By the time I get there, the surprise and embarrassment has morphed into red hot anger. I whirl around to find Cam standing behind me, his hands in his pockets, a sheepish look on his face.

"I'm so sorry about that," Cam says, his sincerity causing me to falter momentarily. I get over it quickly.

"Don't be," I say, the words coming sharp as daggers. "I should have known you'd end up with Ainsley eventually."

He narrows his eyes at me. "What's that supposed to mean?"

The sun has set, and a chill has settled over the night air. I slip on my jacket and wrap my arms around myself, taking my time thinking of a good answer to his question.

"She always wanted you in high school. Looks like she finally got you."

He scowls, and I feel a little bit like a petulant teenager throwing something from high school in his face. The several drinks I've had, however, are doing their job and making me feel way more confident and self-assured than normal. When he doesn't respond, I quip, "I just thought you were a better guy than that, that's all."

"Again, what's *that* supposed to mean?"

The words are practically a growl, and the intensity of the disdain in his voice sobers me right up. Too late now, though.

"She's awful, and you're not. Or I guess, I thought you weren't. I don't know." My words are choppy and confused as I wage a battle with the sudden nervousness and humiliation that have taken over my brain. Nervousness, because I've now gone down a rabbit hole. Humiliation, because for the briefest moment back in the bar, I'd wondered if there could be a sliver of a second chance for Cam and I. *You sad, sorry idiot.*

"People change, Lizzie," he says, his voice a low, soft rumble.

"Yeah, I can see that."

We stand in silence by my car for a beat, the wind picking up and causing me to shiver. The thing about being right on the coast in the Northeast is that no matter how warm it is during the day, the nights can be bitter with enough wind. Cam notices my chattering teeth and takes a step toward me, his arm outstretched as if he is going to touch me, warm me up. I shrink away from him, despite how appealing I might have found the gesture earlier in the evening.

"I should go," I say, opening my car door and sliding into the driver's seat. Cam nods and jams his hands back into his pockets, merely watching as I start the car, pull out of the parking lot, and drive off into the night.

I barely put the car in park in Gran's driveway before I whip my phone out and dial Trisha's number. At first, she's surprised that I'm calling her so late, and I realize that it's almost 11 o'clock on a Thursday night. Most adults my age are asleep at this time of night, since they have adult things to attend to the next day, like kids and work. *Not me,* my slightly buzzed brain thinks. *You're a husbandless, childless spinster. Heck, maybe you'll even be jobless too, depending how long you have to spend in this God-forsaken town.*

Working hard not to cry or slur my words, I explain to Trisha the events of the night, starting with my sort-of-date with Cam and ending with the very unexpected encounter with Ainsley, and the news that she and Cam had recently been an item. I am met with a long, lofty silence.

Great, she thinks I'm absolutely nuts.

To my surprise, Trisha simply says, "Don't move, I'll be right over."

Not fifteen minutes later, Trisha is at the door in her pajamas with two bottles of wine, a party-size bag of potato chips, a box of brownies, and a small stack of DVDs. I stand there, stunned, as she pushes past me and into the living room, setting the supplies on the coffee table and immediately inspecting the television set up.

"I hope Helen has a DVD player, I sold all my VHS tapes at a garage sale before I moved in with Eddie," she says matter-of-factly, peering into the TV stand. She lets out a long sigh when she locates the DVD player, and pops in one of the discs she brought with her.

"What are you doing?" I ask, still standing by the door, both intrigued and a little frightened. "Are we going to watch sappy movies or something?"

Trisha barks a laugh.

"First, we're going to watch Carrie," she explains, a devilish grin on her face. "And down a bottle of wine while you tell me all about what happened. Then, once we're all done venting, we'll put on some sappy movies and have a good cry. That's what the brownies and second bottle of wine are for."

Makes sense, I think, feeling both grateful and a little frightened. "I'll go get us some wine glasses."

I find some wine glasses in the kitchen and take them back out to the living room, where Trisha has the movie ready to go, the wine bottle cracked, and pillows and blankets laid out on the couch. She shoos me away to go put my pajamas on, which I quickly do in the powder room and then get settled on the couch. Trisha pours us generous glasses of wine, presses play on the movie, and then turns to me.

"So," she says, "spill."

The serenely creepy opening theme music to Carrie begins to play, an oddly appropriate soundtrack to my jumbled feelings about Cam and Ainsley.

"I'm an idiot, that's all there is to spill," I say, but Trisha shakes her head.

"You're not an idiot. If anything, Cam's the idiot. I will never understand why he dated Ainsley in the first place," she says fervently, clearly hoping to make me feel better. It's not working.

"To make up for lost time?" I say, biting back the lump forming in my throat. "She always hated me in high school, always told me she could never understand how the captain of the football team would pick a nobody nerd like me over the head cheerleader. As if it were impossible that life would be like anything *other* than a crappy teen movie."

Trisha winces. "We were really awful back then," she says, referring to her role in Ainsley's posse of popular girls. "I'm so sorry."

"It's ancient history," I tell her, even though I know that's a lie. "Ainsley was always trying to get us to break up. I guess I'm not surprised that she made a move on Cam, seeing as she succeeded and all. Even if it was ten years later."

"From what I heard, it only lasted a few weeks before Cam broke it off," Trisha says, the glint in her eye telling me she has the scoop. She gives me a sly smile, and despite how terrible I'm feeling, I find I'm kind of dying to hear about it.

"What else did you hear?" I ask, suddenly grateful for small-town gossip.

"Apparently, Cam doesn't do commitment," she tells me. "He dates someone for a few weeks, and then right as things start to get serious, he breaks it off. Ainsley was convinced Cam was 'the one,' but he just called her up out of the blue one day and said that they were going in different directions and he needed to work on himself."

"How do you know all this?" I ask, shocked at how much Trisha has told me.

"Ainsley owns the hair salon in town, and that place is the beating heart of the town's gossip mill."

Ahh. How fitting.

"According to Ainsley, they will get back together any day now. It's just a matter of time. But if you ask me..." her face softens, and she looks directly into my eyes. "There's a past love he just hasn't quite gotten over."

A chill races through me, and I can feel my face getting flushed. I drain my glass of wine, and hold the empty glass out to Trisha for a re-fill, saying nothing. Trisha laughs, and then adds, "By the looks of it, neither have you."

I wrinkle my nose, but still don't say anything. It doesn't change the fact that the thought of Cam and Ainsley together, of Cam picking her up for a date, holding her hand, kissing her... the thought of all that twists my stomach into knots, the same way it did when I was a teenager. The thought of anything beyond that makes me want the ground to swallow me up and spit me out into the void. No, it doesn't matter what unresolved feelings either one of us might have about the past. We couldn't possibly go there again. Not now.

I look at the television screen, where Carrie is being forced into a closet by her mother after being humiliated by her classmates and dismissed from school, and figure I can understand why the movie ends the way it does.

• • • •

THE NEXT MORNING, I wake up to a loud banging noise that seems to shake the entire house. I peel myself off the couch, my head feeling like it weighs a thousand pounds, and pick up a handwritten note off the coffee table.

Had to open the store today. Hope you feel better! Let's talk later.
-Trish

"How?" I say aloud, wincing as the sound of my own voice sends a sharp pain up the left side of my skull. After killing both bottles of wine and then dipping to Gran's liquor cabinet last night, I can't imagine how Trish can stand, let alone go to work. Either she's made of steel, or I can't hold my alcohol anymore. I make a mental note to remember to do something nice for her, to thank her for coming to my rescue.

The banging starts again, the sound like someone is hammering a nail directly into my head. Wondering what it could possibly be, I quickly throw on the same clothes I wore the day before, toss my tangled hair into a ponytail, and run out of the front door, my hands covering my ears and my head splitting.

The light from the morning sun is not my friend. For a moment, I am blinded when I step outside, the rapid adjustment of my pupils setting my brain on fire, a wave of nausea crashing over me. I come to a screeching halt on the porch, bracing my hands on my thighs, and hanging my head low between my legs. I inhale a few deep breaths, trying to get my bearings, noticing that in addition to the banging, I can also hear the dull chatter of people talking and the sound of power tools. Once I am confident that I won't vomit all over the porch, I slowly raise my head and stand up, jumping backward when I see Cam standing over me.

"Morning," he says, his head cocked to the side and a silly grin on his face. I can't imagine what he's smiling about so damn early in the morning. It takes me a moment, but I remember that I'm angry with him.

"What are you doing here?" I ask curtly, and he just stares at me. I blink a few times, wincing in pain again at how bright it is. I'm also acutely aware that I look like I've been hit by a truck.

"Your roof," he says, watching intently as I bite back another wave of nausea. A cold sweat breaks out over me, and he asks, "Are you okay?"

"Peachy," I say shakily, exhaling slowly and rubbing my temples. "You're working on the roof already?"

"Well, we got the materials in, and I know you're hoping to get back to New York as soon as possible," Cam replies. "Figured we better get started."

My skin pricks at the idea that he expects me to get out of Rocky Point so soon. *Maybe he just can't wait for me to leave,* I think. Although, after last night, I'm not exactly wanting to stick around to see more of him and Ainsley together. My eyes cross as another wave of nausea crests over me, and I bite back the bile rising in my throat. *Damn wine.*

"Are sure you're okay?" Cam asks.

"I just overdid it a little last night, that's all."

Cam cocks one eyebrow. "I didn't think you had that much to drink."

"Maybe not at the bar," I say scowling at him. "Trisha came over after with some wine to help me forget how much of an idiot I am."

Ignoring my jab, he knits his brows together. "Do you mean Trisha Dodd? I didn't know you two were friends."

"She's Trisha Dearing now," I remind him. "And yes, we are."

"Surprising," he quips. I narrow my eyes at him.

"Well, what can I say? People change."

His eyes darken as I throw his own words back at him, his face softening. Looking around, he takes a step toward me and bends his head close, his voice a low rumble.

"I really am sorry about last night," he says, causing my heart to skip a beat. I can smell the sharp, clean scent of his soap and cologne, the dark blue pools of his eyes bearing into my own. I can tell he's sincere, but I steel my nerves. I'm not some teenager he can charm the pants off anymore. *Sort of.*

"It's fine," I say, trying my best to appear unaffected.

"It's not," he insists. "Look, Ainsley and I dated for a minute, but it ended practically right away. It didn't take long for me to realize she hasn't changed at all. She's manipulative and self-centered, and I didn't want anything to do with it. She took it pretty hard, obviously."

Hello, ego. "You don't owe me an explanation, Cam," I say.

"But I feel like I do. It wasn't even a blip on the radar, Lizzie," he says. "Seriously, there was nothing physical, either."

"Okay, okay," I say, holding up my hands in front of me. *Sheesh, I really didn't need to know that.* "Like I said, you don't need to explain your relationship to me. Who you date is your business."

I fold my arms over my chest and drop my eyes to the ground, chastising myself for the tiny spark of satisfaction I felt when he told me they hadn't done anything physical. It really had been just a short, meaningless fling. Trisha had been right.

Cam clears his throat and jams his hands into his pockets, his eyes flitting from me, then to the ground, then back to me. They settle on my mouth and he licks his lips absentmindedly, causing all the air to disappear from my lungs in an instant. *Oh man, I am in so much trouble.* In a low, steady voice, he says, "When I first saw you, that day in the rain, I didn't know how I would react. Part of the reason why I went over myself after Trisha called was because I needed to see... I needed to know..."

"Know what?" I whisper. His eyes search mine, and he's close enough that I can feel his ragged, unsteady breathing. My heart feels like it's about to jump out of my chest.

"I needed to know if..."

"Boss?"

As if a current of electricity had just shocked us both, Cam and I each jump a full step backward. One of the guys on his crew is standing a few feet away, a bright yellow hardhat on his head and a clipboard in his hand.

"What's up, Hank?" Cam asks.

"Need you to take a look at something, if you don't mind."

Cam shoots a glance back my way, then nods at Hank. "Sure thing."

He follows Hank around to the back of the house, and I exhale a long, slow breath. Head still pounding, I go back inside where I find that my cell phone is on the coffee table, blinking with a notification. I click the button on the side of my phone to unlock the screen, and see that I have five missed calls, four voicemails, and several text messages, all from Cheryl. The most recent text message simply reads: *SOS. Get here, now.*

My stomach knots at the sight of the message, and I immediately dial Cheryl back, trying not to panic. *Please, please pick up*, I think as the phone rings and rings, three times, then four, then five, until an exasperated Cheryl finally comes on the other side of the phone.

"Elizabeth," she says, sounding slightly out of breath, as though she's been running a marathon. "You've got to get to the nursing home, quick. Your grandmother is... well, she's having an episode."

"An episode?" I ask, grabbing my purse and car keys and heading back outside. "What kind of episode?"

"I'll explain when you get here, just... come quick."

The other end of the line clicks before I can get another word in, and I swallow hard. Jogging off the porch, I head toward my car, visions of worst-case scenarios running through my head. I don't know enough about Gran's disease to know what Cheryl meant by 'episode,' but I assume it can't be good. My tunnel vision causes me to run straight into something solid, and... warm? I shake myself out of it and look up to see a broad chest in front of me, large arms holding onto mine, the contact practically searing my skin.

It's Cam.

"Lizzie, what the hell? Where are you going?" he asks.

"No time," I say, shaking my head. I realize the rest of me is shaking, too. "I have to get to Gran."

"Gran? Is something wrong with Helen? Lizzie, talk to me!"

Cam's hands come up to my shoulders, and he bends down until he's eye-level with me. I suck in a deep breath, staring into his dark blue eyes as if they're the only thing keeping me rooted to the ground.

"Cheryl said I need to get there fast," I choke out, swallowing the lump in my throat. "I don't... I don't know what's going on, but it doesn't sound good."

"Okay," he says, his thumbs gently rubbing my arm. The contact sends an explosion of goosebumps over my skin. "Take a deep breath. I'll go with you, just give me one second."

"No," I say. I can't make him go with me to deal with Gran, especially not knowing what I'm about to walk into. I can't burden him with this. "I'm fine, really."

"You're not fine," Cam insists. "Let me tell my crew I'll be stepping out for a little while, and I'll drive you."

His gives my shoulders a little squeeze, and my heart squeezes, too. I want to tell him no, make him stay, but I'm feeling panicky and my legs are wobbly. Deep down, I'm grateful for the offer.

"Okay," I say. "Thank you."

"Of course," he says, releasing me. My arms immediately miss the warmth of his hands. He turns back to the house and his crew. "Hank!" he yells. "I need to head out for a little while. Call my cell if you need me."

"Sure thing, boss!" Hank yells back. His hand coming to the small of my back, Cam guides me to his truck, which I hadn't noticed was parked in the driveway until now. He opens the passenger door and I climb into the cab of the truck, buckling my seatbelt as he jogs around to the driver's side and gets in.

Cam starts the truck and peels out of the driveway, heading out of Rocky Point proper toward the nursing home. We sit in silence on the drive, Cam's knuckles white on the steering wheel. I'm looking out the window, watching the trees and houses pass by. Despite the fact that I'm anxious about the unknown, and what the future might look like for Gran, I feel comforted that Cam is beside me. His presence is like a security blanket, letting me know that I'm not alone in this, and I am thankful.

Chapter Ten

Elizabeth

I PRACTICALLY LAUNCH myself out of the car when we get to the nursing home, Cam trailing closely behind me. He hangs back when we get to Gran's apartment, muttering that he doesn't want to intrude but also giving me a look that says, *if you need me, I'm here.* I can hear commotion from inside the apartment, and my heart is ready to burst from my chest, the sound of my heartbeat echoing like a drumline. I give Cam one last look, one that I hope says *thank you,* and then hastily turn the doorknob to Gran's apartment and step inside.

I'm barely inside the threshold when something small and heavy sails past my face, hitting the wall to my right and shattering on impact. I duck instinctively, and look around to see Cheryl by Gran's bedroom, peeking around the open door. In the kitchenette, nurse Angie is tending to a male aide with a gash on his head, holding a towel to the open, bleeding wound. I observe the scene for a brief moment, dumbstruck, before I can comprehend what's happening. Gran has clearly gone postal.

"What the hell is going on in here?" I ask, getting Cheryl's attention. She looks crazed, but relieved to see me, and darts past the door as if she's running from heavy enemy fire.

"The crazy old bird clocked me over the head when I tried to administer her meds!" the aide shouts. My mouth drops open in disbelief. I know Gran has always been a tough cookie, but I can't imagine her being intentionally violent to anyone. Not physically, anyway. Angie scowls at the aide, who can't be more than twenty years old, and swats him on the arm.

"Don't you call her names, Stuart. She is scared and agitated, it's not her fault."

"Tell that to my bleeding head!" he shouts back, and Angie takes his hand and presses it over the towel on his head.

"Apply some pressure and don't move, you'll be fine!" she yells, jogging over to Cheryl and I by the front door.

"Get out of my house!" Gran shrieks from the bedroom, another object flying out from the doorway. This time, it's a hard plastic water cup. Water and ice sail through the air, soaking the carpet. "He's trying to poison me!"

"I'm not trying to poison you!" Stuart shouts back. Cheryl, Angie, and I turn and scowl at him. Stuart frowns and sits down on one of the kitchen chairs, his hand still pressed firmly on the towel against his head. Angie then turns to me.

"It's the dementia," Angie explains, calmer than I would expect her to be. "It's not uncommon for the patient to exhibit aggressive or paranoid behaviors as the disease progresses. In this case, she got scared and took it out on poor Stuart over there."

I hear her, but I'm hung up on something she said. "Disease... *progresses?*" I ask, and Angie nods solemnly.

"Unfortunately, yes. The dementia may be farther along than the doctor initially thought. You have to understand, she doesn't recognize anyone right now. We're all strangers, and all she knows is that Stuart was trying to make her take pills. Can you imagine how terrifying that would be?"

I swallow hard and nod, the knot in my stomach tightening. Just then, the door to the apartment opens, and Cam sticks his head in.

"I heard a lot of commotion," he says. "Everything okay?"

Angie and Cheryl turn to me, their eyebrows raised, as if to say, *who on earth is that?* He nods a greeting at them, then turns his attention back to me.

"Everything is fine," I say, as an object flies past the back of my head and smacks against the wall. I look and see that it was a shoe. Cam's face scrunches, and he cocks an eyebrow.

"You sure about that?" he steps through the door and closes it behind him, and I watch as Cheryl and Angie slowly look him up and down, their mouths dropping open slightly. I don't blame them; Cam's tall, broad stature and chiseled features are definitely a sight to behold. Maybe it's the craziness of this day, but I'm just now realizing how *good* he looks, in his faded jeans and a black crew neck t-shirt that stretches over the peaks and valleys of his muscular, defined chest and shoulders. He clears his throat, and I realize we're all just staring at him.

"Gran isn't having a good day," I say, another shoe flying out into the small room. "Her dementia has gotten worse."

Cam lets out a low whistle. "Okay, so what do we need to do?"

"Don't worry about it," I say, to which Cheryl and Angie whip their heads around to stare at me. "We got this."

"We do?" Cheryl asks. "I don't think we got this."

"Yeah, I think we could use the help of a..." Angie looks Cam up and down again. "A big, strong man."

Stuart grumbles in the background, and Angie shoots him another death glare.

I roll my eyes at both of them, and Cam smiles wide. "I'm happy to help."

"It's *fine*, really," I insist, but Cheryl ignores me and grabs Cam by the arm, pulling him toward the door and using him like a giant human shield. Gran has grown quiet, and there are no more projectiles being launched from the bedroom. Even though I think this is a horrible idea, I jog up next to Cam, and together we creep closer to the bedroom door. We wait a beat, not wanting to scare Gran.

"Is someone out there?" she asks shakily, and my heart breaks into a million pieces. She must be so confused and scared, not knowing where she is, or why, and thinking someone has broken in or is trying to hurt her in some way. I clear my throat and shoot a sideways glance at Cam.

"It's me, Gran. It's Elizabeth," I call out.

"Who?" Gran asks, and I watch as Cam's eyes, still bearing into mine, soften at Gran's lack of recognition. It stings, but I try again.

"Your granddaughter," I say. "Can I come in?"

Gran doesn't respond, so I creep closer to the open door and poke my head inside the bedroom. Gran is standing next to her bed in a pale-blue, cotton nightgown, her eyes wide and her hands wrapped around one of her slippers. She spots me and her hands twitches on the slipper, her lip quivering. I put my hands up in a *don't shoot* gesture, inching further into the room.

"It's me, gran. Elizabeth. Do you remember?"

She shakes her head, her grip tightening on the slipper. Her eyes widen, and I see Cam out of the corner of my eye, sideling up next to me. I elbow him hard.

"What are you doing?" I mutter, but he doesn't respond. I look back to Gran, who is laser focused on Cam. Her eyes flit from him, to me, and back to Cam.

"Mrs. Quinn?" Cam asks. Gran looks stricken, but can't take her eyes off of him. "Helen, can you put the slipper down?"

Carefully, she bends down and puts the slipper on the floor, her eyes never leaving Cam. When she straightens, she looks back at me again, her eyes filling with tears.

"Elizabeth?" she asks, in a low whisper. I nod, and take a few steps closer to her.

"Yes, Gran," I breathe. "It's me, I'm here."

I sit down on the edge of the bed, and she does, as well. She looks back up at Cam, who hasn't moved from his spot in the doorway. I watch as she tilts her head to one side, recognition dawning over her.

"Cameron?" she asks. My mouth drops open, and Cam flashes her a brilliant smile.

"Hi, Mrs. Q," he says, a boyish lilt to his voice that I haven't heard in almost a decade. Gran scrunches her brows together, then turns back to me.

"I'm very tired," she says. "I'd like to lie down."

"Yes, of course Gran," I say, helping her into bed. Once she is settled, the covers tucked up to her chest, I ask, "Can Stuart come in and give you your medicine now? He tried earlier, but you... you weren't ready for your medicine."

"I'm not coming anywhere near that room!" Stuart grumbles, and I hear a loud *swat*, what sounds like a rolled-up magazine or newspaper striking him. "Hey!"

"Let me do it," Angie says, striding into the room with the pill cup and a fresh glass of ice water, the issue of Better Home and Garden rolled up under her arm.

"That would be all right," Gran says, nodding.

I wait with her as Angie gives her the medicine, and then sit with Gran for a few more minutes until she is relaxed and resting. Once she is asleep, I look up at Cam, who hasn't moved from his post by the door, tears filling my eyes and threatening to spill over.

"Thank you."

• • • •

WE MAKE THE DRIVE BACK to Gran's house in silence. I am still trying to process what happened, Gran's behavior, and the looming progression of her dementia. It's no secret to anyone that my relationship with my grandmother has been a cold one. But the look of fear in her eyes? The pleading, desperate cry for help I saw in her eyes? I am rattled to the core.

To me, Gran has always been the strong, silent pillar of consistency in my life, an anchor to what little family I have on this earth. I knew that raising me was hard on her, in more ways than one. Being a single parent is tough, but a single grandparent? That couldn't have been easy. Add in the fact that I was a walking reminder of my drug-addict mother and criminal father, and well... anyone would struggle with that.

It was tough on me, though, as well. I had no memories of either of my parents, but I knew their sins well. Gran never failed to remind me of how much of a loser my father was, and how he corrupted my mother, her good girl, with drugs and alcohol. She constantly told me how if

I wasn't careful, I would end up just like them. When I let loose even a little bit, and the times were few and far between, mostly consisting of being out a little past curfew, Gran acted as though I'd done something unimaginably horrible. At the time, I felt trapped. Gran's constant persecutions and threats of ending up just like my parents made me want to run so far away, I had spent the last year of high school practically dreaming of the day I could leave town. When the day came, I did so without hesitation. Looking back, I should have checked in on Gran more often. Then again, she should have checked in on me, too. I didn't get Christmas or birthday cards; I didn't get a call. At the time, I figured she was relieved to have me out of her life. No more constant reminder of her failures as a parent. Now, though, all I can think about is the amount of time we lost. The amount of time we'll continue to lose with her illness.

"You doing okay?"

Cam's voice wrenches me from my thoughts, and I turn to look at him. One of the things I'm still trying to wrap my head around is how Gran recognized him. She hadn't recognized me when she first saw me, but when she saw Cam... it was like her memory had suddenly been jogged.

"Did you think that was weird?" I ask, only partially verbalizing my thoughts. Cam gives me a sideways glance.

"Do I think what was weird?"

"How Gran recognized you," I say. "She didn't recognize me, but when she saw you, it was like she started to put the pieces together."

Cam shrugs, turning into Gran's driveway and putting the truck in park. We both unbuckle our seatbelts, but neither one of us moves to get out.

"Have you seen my grandmother much over the last few years?" I ask, and Cam shakes his head.

"Nope. I've maybe run into her at the grocery store a time or two. Can't say I've seen her much beyond that, though."

"Huh," I muse. "How on earth did seeing you bring her back to reality, then?"

Cam looks at me, a smirk tugging at the corner of his lips. "Maybe it wasn't *me*," he says, emphasizing the last word.

"What do you mean?"

"Maybe it was *us*."

Us. The word reverberates through me like a bolt of electricity. I suppose that Cam and I together could have jogged Gran's memory, seeing as most of the memories she would have of me before moving away would also include Cam. But in her memories, we would be so much younger. Would that matter? I smile at the thought of younger Cam, always wearing a football jersey or some sort of athletic gear, and how much he's changed since we were kids. The amount of thinking I've been doing about Cam and I lately, past and present, cannot be healthy.

"Well, thank you for going with me. I'm sorry to have taken up most of your morning," I say, opening the door and starting to slide out. The feeling of his warm, calloused hands on my arm cause me to freeze. It's a light, gentle touch. One that simply says, *wait*. I turn to look at him, and see his face has suddenly grown profoundly serious.

"Are you sure you're okay?" he asks. I nod, giving him a weak smile. Mostly, I'm tired. I have a full docket of things to accomplish today, but after the morning I've had, I think I need a nap.

"I'm good," I say. "Promise."

"Would you like some company tonight?" he asks, gripping the back of his neck. The question takes me off guard. Company? Like, him?

"What did you have in mind?" I ask, hesitant.

"I don't know, we can find something to do. I just figured that you got some crappy news about your Gran today, you might want to take your mind off of it. I have some things to finish up back at the office, but I should be free around six."

I consider his offer, the only thought coming to mind a memory of the way his fingers felt against my skin just now. I should say no. I should thank him for coming to my rescue, *again*, get out of the truck, and leave it at that. But something about the way he's looking at me, the way his walls have suddenly come down, makes it impossible to say no. In typical Cam fashion, he read me like an open book. The last thing I want is to be alone tonight, after everything that happened today. I had thought for a moment about calling Trisha, and seeing if she wanted to watch the rest of those movies. But then Cam made his offer, and honestly, nothing could sound *more* appealing. I tuck a loose strand of hair that has fallen out of my ponytail behind my ear, and give him the friendliest smile I can muster.

"Six it is," I say, and I'm rewarded with a gigantic grin that makes my heart race.

"Okay, but be ready for *anything*," he says, giving me a pointed look. Heat pricks at the back of my neck as my mind wanders at the suggestion, images of Cam and I alone intruding into my thoughts. My cheeks redden almost instantly.

"Anything?" I ask, the wariness obvious in my voice. He winks at me.

"Just trust me. Keep an open mind."

"I will try my best," I say. "Should I be worried?"

"That depends entirely on your sense of adventure," he says, releasing me so that I can slide out of the truck. Once I'm planted firmly on the ground, I close the door and watch as he pulls out of the driveway and leaves, my cheeks still burning from my inappropriate daydreaming.

It's not my sense of adventure that I'm worried about, so much as my ability to resist that man's charm. I thought I'd gotten over the whole lovesick teenager act, but apparently, I was mistaken. Apparently, Cam still has the same effect on me as he did when we were kids. And if I'm not careful, I might find myself right back where I started with Cameron Tate.

• • • •

AT SIX O'CLOCK SHARP, I pull up outside of Tate Construction's main offices and park in one of the open spots, hoping Cam doesn't see me arriving exactly right on time. Stupid, I know, but as I went through the motions of my day, contacting Gran's lawyer and getting appointments set up for early next week, my mind kept wandering to Cam and how excited I was to spend time with him. I knew it would take about ten minutes to get to his office, and at 5:50 I had raced to my car and set out. Now, as I'm sitting in front of the building at six on the dot, I'm wondering if I should hang in the car for a few minutes, pretend to be fashionably late. I wouldn't want Cam to think I'm looking forward to this, or anything.

A knock on my driver's side window startles me, causing me to practically jump into the passenger seat. I look up, and Cam is standing outside my car, looking down at me, grinning like a damn fool. He motions for me to get out of the car, a backpack thrown over his shoulder and a baseball cap turned backward on his head.

So much for that.

I climb out of the car and adjust my top, a silky, olive green sleeveless V-neck with lace detailing around the neckline. I'd decided to pair it with skinny jeans and tan strappy sandals, going for a casual yet cute look for the evening's yet-to-be-determined activities. The color of the shirt played nicely off my olive skin tone and eye color, and I felt super cute and just a tad sexy when I finished getting ready. I wanted a look that Cam would notice, but that wouldn't look like I tried too hard. Cam takes me in, his eyes settling on the lace detail of my top, and his face scrunches.

If there's anything that can take your confidence from 100 to zero in a matter of milliseconds, it's the look Cam is giving my outfit right now.

"That's what you're wearing?" he asks, and my mouth drops open in shock.

"Excuse me?" I ask, thinking I must be hallucinating.

"I told you to be ready for anything," he says, a smirk tugging at the corner of his mouth. I can feel heat pricking at the back of my neck, and I wring my hands in front of me.

"So? What's wrong with my outfit?"

He shakes his head, removing his baseball cap and running his hands through his hair. "Nothing. We should get going, though. We'll want as much daylight as possible."

As much daylight as possible? My curiosity piques as I follow him to his truck, observing what he's wearing, my stomach sinking. He has on silky black basketball shorts, a gray t-shirt, sneakers, and his baseball cap.

"So, what's the plan?" I ask, trying to conceal the concern in my voice. He looks back and me and chuckles.

"Still a surprise," he says. He rounds to the passenger side of his truck and opens the door, holding it open while I climb inside. It's a sweet gesture, and I remember that he always used to hold doors open for me back when we were... well, back *then*. When he gets into the driver's side, I turn to face him.

"Holding the door open, nice touch," I say. "I guess chivalry isn't dead."

He winks at me and starts the car. "Old habits die hard, I guess."

My stomach flutters, a slow smile spreading across my face.

"Did you get everything done today that you needed to?" he asks, and I nod.

"For the most part. Gran's lawyer won't be able to meet with me until Monday, and the bank is closed over the weekend, so I'll have to wait until next week to take care of a lot of it. For now, though, I feel like I got a lot accomplished."

"Excellent. Well, I hope you're ready for some fun because I have a pretty cool evening lined up for us," Cam says. There's that word, again. *Us.* I let it hang in the air between us, enjoying the cool breeze of the bright spring evening as we drive north toward the bay and Rocky Point Harbor. Within minutes, the gray and blue expanse of Cape Cod bay comes into view. Some sailboats are still out taking advantage of the day's generous winds, their sails colorful, the scene reminiscent of a painting. I sigh as we pull into the marina, an unexpected thought crossing my mind *You don't get views like this back in New York City.*

Cam must be able to sense my thoughts, because he turns off the car, turns to me, and says, "Probably not the kind of Friday night you'd get in New York, huh?"

I laugh, unbuckling my seatbelt. "No, definitely not."

The marina is the beating heart of Rocky Point, functioning as both a center of commerce and a tourist attraction. Fisherman and crabbers offload their catches to businesses and passersby alike from their boats or makeshift booths on the docks, and the bars and restaurants surrounding the marina boast fresh seafood and unobstructed views of the bay, drawing a crowd most nights. We make our way down to the docks, the wind whipping up the closer we get to the water. I trail a few steps behind Cam, surprised when we stop abruptly in front of a docked center-console fishing boat with the name *Sid's Sea Maiden* emblazoned on the side in curly red lettering. He turns to face me and holds up a hand toward the boat.

I take a step back, my eyes widening. Cam looks back at me, his eyes full of mirth, and points to the boat.

"So, what do you think?" he asks, climbing on board. "Isn't she a beauty?"

I drop my hands to my sides, staring at it, thinking there is no way we're about to get on that thing.

"Is this your boat?" I ask.

"No, we're hijacking it. Of course it's my boat, now hurry up and climb on. I told you we want as much daylight as possible."

He reaches out a hand to help me on, but I try to maneuver my way onboard without it. Hands on his hips, he watches as I straddle the stern, one foot on the dock and one on the deck of the boat. I'm wobbly, but I throw my full weight toward the boat anyway, bringing my other leg on board and promptly losing my balance. Just as I'm sure I'm about to eat the deck of the boat, a pair of large, strong arms envelop me and root me to the ground. I stay completely still, worried that if I move even half an inch backward, I'm going to back right into Cam's broad, muscular chest, tight abs, and... well, I try not to think about anything *south* of his abs, otherwise I might spontaneously combust.

"You alright?" he asks, letting his hands linger on my hips even though I'm now firmly planted on the ground.

"We'll see," I breathe. I'm not so sure.

Chapter Eleven

Cameron

NOTE TO SELF: WHEN you tell a girl to be ready for anything, she's not going to know that you mean, *be ready to potentially, maybe, go on an impromptu fishing trip.* Sure, that's my bad. But now that we're actually on the boat, and she's wearing that lacy top and those tight jeans that look like they may as well have been painted on... well, I'm starting to second guess my own plan.

"So, what's the plan?" she asks, her voice hesitant but hopeful. I look around at the cooler full of beer and tackle box full of bait next to two fishing poles, and suddenly feel like this was a *terrible* idea.

"Okay," I say, gripping the back of my neck and shaking my head. "Don't laugh, but I thought we could go fishing."

I watch as her eyes widen, and she tries as hard as she possibly can to keep her face straight. She always used to do that when we were together, try her best to spare my feelings, coddle my ego. Despite how much I feel like an idiot, I'm oddly comforted that she's still trying not to hurt my feelings.

"Sounds great," she says, slowly and evenly. She's trying so hard, and she's a saint for it. I shake my head and let out a nervous laugh.

"It was a stupid idea. This is just what I do whenever I'm feeling stressed or overwhelmed, and since *you're* feeling stressed and overwhelmed..." Lizzie gives me a sincere if sympathetic smiles, and I drop my eyes to the ground. "See? Stupid idea."

"It's not stupid," she says. "It's actually kind of sweet."

"I appreciate you saying that, but I promise, my ego can take it. We can do something else."

"No," she says firmly, planting her hands on her hips. I let my gaze follow them, swallowing hard. Damn, she looks good. Why the hell did I think this would be a good idea? "Let's go fishing. I think that sounds fun."

"Are you sure?"

"I'm sure. Plus, we're already on the boat."

She has a point there.

I start the boat's engine and untie us from the dock, taking a seat in the console and slowly motoring us out into Cape Cod bay. With a few hours remaining until sunset, the bay is dotted with sailboats, people in kayaks and on paddleboards, and music from the shops and restaurants at the marina carries out onto the water, creating a picture-perfect scene. Farther out into the bay are other fishing boats and a few larger crafts, all enjoying the still waters and clear blue sky. This. *This* is why I wanted to take her out here, to share this little bit of peace that I so often run to when the days get rough, or the darkness creeps back in. Something about the water always lifts my spirits, and I'm guessing that's something she doesn't get enough of back in New York. Rather than sitting down, Lizzie stands next to me, holding onto the back of my seat and staring out at the water, a look of pure excitement on her face. Once we're past the no-wake zone, I turn to face her.

"Hold on tight," I tell her, before I gun the throttle of the boat. She lets out a little squeak of surprise, giggling and holding on tight as we bounce over waves and fly across the bay. When we get out by the other fishing boats, to a nice, deep spot that will be good for dropping anchor and casting out a line, I slow to a stop. I get up to drop the anchor while Lizzie looks around at the deep azure water, a huge smile on her face.

Bingo.

"I hope you like beer," I say, opening up the cooler and twisting open a bottle. I hand one to her and she inspects it for a moment, shrugging.

"I can't remember the last time I had a beer," she says, twisting open the cap and taking a sip.

"Really? What do you typically drink?"

"Vodka sodas," she says. "Or martinis."

Girly drinks. I could have figured that.

She takes another sip of her beer, then frowns and takes a seat on the bench at the stern of the boat. My heart sinks instantly. This was *such* a bad idea.

"Look, we really don't have to go if you don't want to," I say, taking a seat next to her. "Really, I won't be offended."

"It's not that," she says, drawing her legs up onto the bench seat and hugging them against her chest. She looks as though she might cry, and *oh shit*, I am not equipped to deal with this. The plan was to cheer her up, but clearly all I've done is made her feel even worse. I'm not even sure how. I rake a hand through my hair, looking for the right words but coming up empty.

"Was it something I said?"

She shakes her head. "No," she says. "Not directly."

"Then what's wrong?" I ask. She turns to face me, her brows drawn together, a pained look in her eyes.

"Why are you being so nice to me all of a sudden?" she asks, and the question catches me off guard.

"What do you mean?"

"When I first came back into town, you weren't exactly happy to see me. In fact, you were downright... *angry*," she explains. "You were short with me. Cold, even. And as I surprised as I was to see you, your reaction was actually exactly what I would have expected. I *hurt you*, Cam. You should be... I don't know, giving me all kinds of Hell. Making me feel jealous. *Anything* besides being so... nice!"

I can't help it, I smirk at her, which only seems to cause her even more anguish.

"You want me to try to make you jealous?"

"What? No, I don't want you to. I'm just saying I deserve it, is all."

I shake my head. Sure, I'd been surprised to see her and yeah, maybe I hadn't reacted the friendliest. But, I have no desire to make her life a living hell. I don't want to see her jealous. Would it be extremely satisfying for the girl who stomped on my heart to at least feel the teensiest bit of regret? Sure, 100%. But I don't *actively* want to cause her pain. Quite the opposite, actually.

"Plus, there's the whole *Ainsley* thing," she adds, rolling her eyes as she says Ainsley's name. "I acted like a total idiot at Ryan's the other night, getting so mad at you. I had no right."

No right? "What do you mean by that?" I ask.

"Well what did I expect? That you would just never move on? Of course you're going to date, you have every right to date whoever you want. Even..." she scrunches her face in a look of disgust. "*Ainsley.*"

"I have to tell you something."

The words are out of my mouth before I can stop them, the part of my brain that wants so desperately to make her feel better taking over. I'm probably going to regret it, but I swallow hard and steel my nerves anyway.

"Okay," she says, her eyes widening in alarm.

"I thought dating Ainsley would make me feel better. It doesn't make a lot of sense, but I thought that if I dated Ainsley, it would be like evening the score, in a way."

I watch as she processes what I've just said. Speaking the words out loud had made me want to cringe, so I can only imagine what she thought of it. She folds her hands in her lap and sits quietly, her eyes darting back and forth as it sinks in. Because I'm an utter idiot, I keep going.

"I knew that for whatever reason, Ainsley was always trying to get between us in school. I always told you it was nothing back then, because I only had eyes for you. But I knew to an extent that it was true, and that you both hated each other. Well one day a few months back, I was hanging out at Ryan's with some guys from work, we'd just finished up a job, and Ainsley walked in. We started talking, somehow got on the topic of high school, and she owned up to it. Admitted everything. She told me she had a crush on me, but I was never available, and she thought it was crazy that the captain of the football team would date a nobody," I say, adding, "Her words, not mine."

Lizzie winces, but doesn't say anything. She doesn't look at me. I continue.

"She even owned up to that day. Told me that you'd begged her not to say anything. She felt guilty, Lizzie. She apologized to me. And I don't know why, but I felt like the universe was playing some cruel fucking joke. You'd moved on, Ainsley had apologized for driving a wedge between us, and there I was, still being a miserable prick that couldn't get over it. All I could think of, in that moment, was how pissed you'd be if you saw us together in that bar. So I asked her out on a date."

Lizzie's head whips toward me, her eyes wide and slightly glassy. I suck in a breath, not wanting to upset her any further, and wanting her to just say something, *anything*.

"So you went out with Ainsley to get back at me?" she asks, her voice just above a whisper.

"Basically," I say, finally owning it out loud. It doesn't help the churning in my stomach, though. Or the fact that I feel like a jerk. "That's why I broke it off so quickly, it wasn't fair to Ainsley. It didn't make me feel any better, either. I realized I had some serious soul-searching to do."

"And then I showed up," she says. I nod my head, the pitiful, pathetic irony making me want to laugh.

"And then you showed up."

She returns her gaze to her lap, where she is wringing her hands together. Her brows are knit together, and I can tell she's deep in thought. I want so badly to know what she's thinking, if she's upset with me, if she's trying to figure out a way to get off this boat and swim back to shore, get as far away from me as she can. I exhale slowly, feeling the weight of the confession lift off my shoulders. Somehow, though, there's still a deep twinge of guilt twisting in my gut.

Lizzie stands up and crosses her arms over her chest, pacing the small deck of the boat. She looks out over the water, her mouth a tight line, and I brace myself for her to demand I take her back to shore.

Instead, and to my surprise, she just throws her hands in the air, and then picks up one of the fishing poles.

"Okay, are we going to do this, or what?"

Chapter Twelve

Elizabeth

I'VE NEVER BEEN GREAT at dealing with things head on. In fact, I'm actually much better at avoiding anything uncomfortable and just hoping it will go away. Case in point: the fact that I *still* haven't gone into my childhood bedroom for fear of whatever gross, ugly feelings it will bring to the surface.

Cam's confession about dating Ainsley to get back at me? Yeah, same deal.

I did what I do best in these situations and changed the subject, deciding to instead focus on fishing. *Fishing.* I've been fishing maybe once in my life, and I can't say it's what I expected Cam's surprise outing to be. But honestly, I'd rather do anything than deal with the roller coaster of emotions I've been feeling ever since he told me about his reason for dating Ainsley. So, I bite the bullet, bait a line, and plop my butt onto the rigid bench seat, proceeding to go fishing for only the second time, ever.

"This is nice," I say, crossing my legs and staring out over the open water. The sky is clear and blue, not a single cloud in sight. *Except*, of course, that cloud of anxiety that's been hanging over me since we first stepped on this boat.

I look over at Cam, who is staring at me with wide eyes and knitted brows, clearly still confused by my abrupt change in subject and demeanor. But it's too late, I made the choice, now I have to commit to it.

"Honestly, I forgot how great the weather is up here this time of year. And the air quality, *so* much cleaner and fresher than New York City," I say, reaching out to jimmy the fishing pole, which is secured into a holder attached to the boat's railing. I don't feel any bites yet, save for that nagging, gnawing feeling at my insides.

"Are you...?" Cam croaks, and I flash him a big smile.

"Am I what? Enjoying fishing? Absolutely."

"I was going to say, 'are you okay?' Because you're acting really fucking weird right now."

I gulp, returning my gaze to my lap. Okay, so he's not going to let this go. Fine. I can be a big girl and talk about this. Inhaling a deep breath, I turn to face him, my heart skipping a little beat at the way he's looking at me with those dark, dangerous eyes. Like he's genuinely concerned. Why does he have to be so darn *good*?

"Look, I just don't really want to talk about it. I'm not good at this."

"At what? Talking? You've been pretty okay at it so far."

I roll my eyes dramatically, causing him to snort a laugh. "At dealing with uncomfortable situations."

"I'm making you uncomfortable?"

This damn stubborn man. "No. You're not making me uncomfortable. The situation is making me uncomfortable."

"Fishing?" he asks, this time just a glint of mischief in his eye. Dammit. Damn him. He's going to make me say it. He hasn't changed one bit.

I swallow hard, wringing my hands together. "The thing with Ainsley. The fact that after all this time, you still want to get back at me for breaking up with you. I'm not sure what it means."

He doesn't answer right away, just nods. I'm not sure I want him to answer, or to clarify what it all means, because it will probably just make things more complicated than they already are. As soon as Gran's house is fixed and on the market, I'm on my way back to New York. I'm playing with fire by letting myself get close to Cam again. The only logical outcome of this is that one or both of us get hurt, but for some reason, I just can't help myself.

"It means I still haven't gotten over it," Cam says, his voice a low rumble that sends chills down my spine, and goosebumps exploding across my skin. "It means I still haven't gotten over you."

I suck in a breath, not sure what to say. He looks at me intently, waiting for me to respond, but my lungs can't find any air to speak.

Raking my clammy hands through my hair, I stand up and start pacing the deck again. Cam stands up, too, but I need to put some distance between us. I just can't do this with him, not now. Even though my heart and my body are screaming at me to just let my guard down, my rational, over-thinking brain can't do it.

"This isn't a good idea, Cam. I thought catching up would be good for us, but clearly it's not going to work."

He takes a few steps toward me, closing the distance between us in two long strides. Heat prickles at my skin, my stomach churning as the silence settles around us, magnified by the gentle rocking of the boat beneath us.

"You're the one who wanted to catch up in the first place," Cam points out, and he's got me there. "I didn't even want to, until I realized I had that picture of you, that first night in the rain, burned into my brain. I didn't think I'd ever see you again, but there you were. I started to wonder, maybe we were getting a second chance. Maybe we could move on from the past."

A second chance. At what? A future together? I can see it flashing before my eyes, Cam scooping me up into his arms and kissing me until I'm breathless, like he used to before it all fell apart. But what kind of future could we have when both of our lives are so separate? His family and his business are in Rocky Point, and my life is back in New York. How could we possibly make something like that work?

I shake my head. "It's too complicated. We're not who we were back then, Cam."

He takes another step toward me, leaving just a few inches between us. He reaches out his hand and his fingers graze mine, heat rippling from my fingertips throughout the rest of my body. His hands feel more calloused than they did before, a result of his years of hard work building his business, literally and figuratively. I wonder what it would feel like to have those rough hands trailing up the exposed skin of my arms, shoulders, neck, the pad of his thumb tracing the line of my jaw.

I shiver at the thought, remembering the feeling of his hands on other parts of me, too. And his lips...

As if he can sense where my mind has wandered, his voice grows husky and pleading. "Maybe we don't have to be."

I could so easily close the last few inches between us and melt into him, uncertain future or complications be damned. Maybe we could just enjoy the time we have together now, and worry about what comes next later. The thought *is* enticing. But what if he's wrong? What if we can't move on from the past?

Before I can decide, the boat abruptly jerks to the right, and I almost lose my balance. We both turn to look at the fishing poles, one of which is now bending over the railing out toward the water, the fishing line taught, as if something is pulling on it hard.

Cam looks me up and down, his mouth twisted into a roguish grin. "To be continued."

We run to the fishing poles and I grab mine, which happens to be the one that's bending over the railing of the boat like it's hooked Cthulhu or something. The moment I take the pole out of the holster on the boat, I am slammed up against the railing as the tension between me and whatever is on the other end of that fishing line turns into an all-out game of tug of war. I brace a heel on the side of the boat while I try to reel it in, while Cam looks in shock out at the water.

"Here, let me help," he says, reaching around me to grab the handle of the fishing pole. I edge him out of the way.

"I got this," I say. "No way I'm letting you reel in the first fish I've ever caught."

"The way that thing is pulling, I'm not so sure it's a fish. At least, not the kind you want to catch," he says, his tone suddenly deadly serious. It only makes me more determined. Plus, this is actually a great way to work out the pent-up tension I'd been feeling just a few moments before.

"If I just... reel it in..."

"I think we should just cut this one loose, Lizzie."

"No way!" I shout, the monster at the other end of the fishing line giving it another tug, sending me straight into the railing again. I try reeling it in a little more. "Clearly this is going to be an epic catch."

"I just think this might be a little dangerous for a first-timer. That thing ain't playing around."

"Second-timer," I correct him, bracing my foot a little higher up on the side of the boat, until it's almost between the side and the rail. "And I've got this!"

I push my foot against the wall, giving myself more leverage to pull on the fishing pole. A large powerboat flies past us, the people on deck watching me grapple with the fishing pole, whooping and hollering at me while I wrestle with the fish from Hell. Their speed creates a wake that begins rocking Cam's boat, and without warning, we crest a small wave and hit the water hard. The boat leans heavily to one side, causing me to lose my footing. Then, it rocks back in the other direction, toward the side that we're standing on, to right itself, and I'm totally unprepared. Cam grabs the railing, bracing himself, but for some reason my hands are glued to the fishing pole. Off balance from the rocking, I don't have time to prepare myself for the pendulum swing back in the other direction. As the side of the boat leans at an impossible angle toward the water, I feel my center of gravity give way, my feet slip, and the fishing pole tugs toward the water, bringing me in a cacophony of flailing arms and legs with it.

I hit the water with a splash, the shock from the icy cold momentarily stunning me. I stay absolutely still as I sink a little, letting myself get oriented and adjust to the temperature. I kick my legs furiously until I bob through the surface of the water, spitting and sputtering and gasping for air. The surprise of the fall still has my adrenaline pumping, and I realize I'm still holding on to the fishing pole, the line of which is no longer tensed but rather sitting on the surface of the water. Whatever demon fish was on the other end of it must have somehow unhooked itself. I let myself bob up and down with the wake, inhaling ragged, salty breaths of air and coughing up ocean water.

Cam leans over the railing of the boat, wide-eyed in shock. I wipe some water out of my eyes, and realize the wake has carried me a few yards away from the boat. Trying not to panic, I start to swim a few strokes toward the ladder at the back of the boat, wanting to get the hell out of the bay as quickly as possible, and fearing that the current might continue to carry me farther away.

"Oh my God, Lizzie!" Cam yells, as if he's finally processed what just happened. "Are you okay?"

"I'm fine," I yell back, the weight of my water-logged jeans causing my progress toward the ladder to be extra slow. My arms and legs are shaky from the shock of the fall, but I use every bit of strength I have to propel myself toward the ladder.

"Stay there, I'm coming in to get you," Cam says, speaking slowly and loudly. "Just stay calm!"

"That's really not necessary," I call back to him, breaking for a moment to catch my breath. Is it just me, or is that ladder getting farther away? Man, I am so out of shape. I try a breast stroke, hoping the movement will give me some better momentum.

"Don't panic, Lizzie. I'm coming!" he yells, causing me to stop again and look up at him.

"I'm good, Cam, I'll be right there!" I yell, but it's too late. I watch as he rips off his baseball cap, hitches his shirt over his head and tosses it onto the boat dock, revealing his tanned, toned chest. I freeze, my eyes taking in the glorious sight of him bare chested, and for a moment I forget to keep kicking. My head dips under the water as another small wave from the wake crests over me, causing me to cough and sputter as I inhale some of the ocean water again.

Great, Lizzie, I think, shaking my head. *Drown yourself at the sight of a half-naked man. That's just great.*

"I'm fine, really," I say, trying again to swim.

"Stay there! I'm coming in for you!"

I look back up at the boat and, *Jesus H Christ*, he's taking off his shorts now. Tight, black boxer briefs sit low on his hips, totally conformed to the shape of his muscular thighs and revealing a noticeable bulge right you-know-where. *Oh, dear God.* My mind momentarily wonders what they look like from the back – in high school, Cam had the cutest butt – and the thought distracts me from yet another small wave that crashes over my face.

Dear Lord. I'm going to die out here if I can't pull it together.

Then again, if he takes off the boxers, I might just drown myself.

Cam leaps off the deck of the boat and plummets into the water, resurfacing quickly and swimming out to me. I watch in awe at the speed and strength of his strokes, finding the seriousness with which he's jumped in to rescue me mildly amusing. I'm not drowning, after all. My clothes are wet, and my pride is hurt, but that's about it. He closes the few yards distance between the boat and I swiftly and easily, thanks to his broad shoulders and impeccably muscular back and chest. I can't help it; I'm mesmerized by the way he moves through the water so easily. Considering how I flopped around like a wet plastic bag trying to make my way back to the boat, his skill in the water is impressive. Hey, maybe I did need rescuing, after all.

When he reaches me, he stops swimming and rubs a hand over his hair and face, brushing away any excess salt water. His skin glistens from the sun hitting the droplets of water covering his face, neck, and shoulders, looking like Goddamned Aquaman or something.

"Are you okay?" he asks.

"Just peachy," I say. "Can we go back to the boat now?"

He smiles a devilish smile, splashing water at me. "You're a stubborn woman, you know that?"

I splash him back. "I am *not*!"

He catches my wrists in his hands, pulling me toward him until I'm tightly against his bare chest, our faces just inches apart. The soaked, exposed fabric of my shirt clings to his skin as well as mine, and I can feel his heat even through the fabric. His touch ignites my body, sending an unexpected shockwave of desire straight to my core. I let out a raggedy breath that incites a slow, sexy smile from Cam.

This is the part where I melt into a puddle of mush and get swept away into the waves, never to be seen again.

Sure, I dated in New York. Nothing was ever serious, but I did have some casual flings. None of them ever felt like the breathless rush of anticipation, the aching, devastating need that Cam elicits from me now with just the slightest bit of skin-to-skin contact. I want to lean into it, into *him*, to get lost in him, but I can't.

"Stubborn," he breathes, his eyes darkening.

He has no idea.

Before I can respond, he moves behind me, enveloping me in his arms and holding me snugly against him. With long, slow kicks he maneuvers us back toward the boat, every single movement of his body rippling against my own, sending pulses of desire through me with every touch. I let the fishing pole, which I'm somehow still holding like it's some kind of lifeline, drag along with us, and pass it to Cam once we are at the ladder. I begin to hoist myself out of the water, and realize with a gasp that I have no change of clothes with me. Panic sets in as I climb back onto the boat, feeling the weight of my soaking wet jeans and the chill of the ocean breeze across my sopping wet skin and shirt. Once I am firmly planted on the boat again, I whirl around, prepared to explain my problem, when I catch him pulling himself out of the water and onto the boat.

He catches me staring at the taught muscles of his arms and broad chest, the rippling six pack and V indentation that starts just above the band of his soaking wet boxers, a devastatingly handsome smile spreading across his face.

"Like what you see?"

Heat pricks at my skin and explodes over my cheeks as I pick my jaw up off the floor. Instinctively, I turn around, as if giving him some privacy, which causes him to laugh. He walks past me and into the center console of the boat, retrieving two big beach towels and tossing one at me. I catch it without making eye contact, and try not to look as he towels himself off.

"I'm going to guess you don't have a change of clothes," he says, as I wrap myself up in the large towel and just stand there, staring at the deck of the boat.

"Erm, no," I mutter.

"I figured," he says, wrapping the towel around his waist and going back into the boat's center console. He fishes around in what looks like a backpack, and pulls out a neatly folded t-shirt and extra pair of basketball shorts. He hands them to me, winking. "Prepared for anything."

"I can see that."

"I'll give you some privacy."

He turns around and crosses his arms across his body, gesturing to the console, the most *privacy* I'm going to get to change on such a small boat. The dampness of my clothes has made me freezing cold, though, so I'll take it. I traipse inside the center console, using the big beach towel for some extra privacy, and carefully take off my sandals, roll off my soaking wet jeans and lift my sopping wet shirt over my head. *Crap*. My bra and undies are also soaking wet, and unless I want the dry clothes he's offered me to get wet too, I'm going to need to remove them. Swallowing hard, I quickly strip them both off, slide on the shorts, and pull the t-shirt over my head. The warm, dry clothes feel a million times better, and I start to relax.

When I go back out onto the deck of the boat, Cam is already dressed in the same shorts and shirt he was wearing. He gives me a once over when he sees me, his eyes darkening for a moment, then laughs.

"Feel better?"

"Much," I say, despite the fact that the shorts are way too big and practically falling off of me. I pulled the drawstring ties as tight as I could, but beggars can't be choosers. I settle onto the bench seat and draw my knees up to my chest, reveling in the warmth of the dry clothes and setting sun. I will never take being warm and dry for granted ever again.

"Are you okay?" he asks, a tone of concern in his voice. I nod my head.

"Yeah, I'm fine."

"I feel awful," he says, shaking his head. "This was supposed to be a fun outing."

"Well, I definitely forgot all my problems for a little while. Mission accomplished," I tease, and he rubs a hand over his eyes.

"Not exactly what I had planned," he says. "You sure you're okay?"

"I'm fine," I insist. And I am. Except the part of me that's supposed to *not* let Cam get back under my skin. That part of me is most certainly not fine.

• • • •

WE GET BACK TO THE marina in record time, the sun now set behind the horizon and the bay basking in a purply, dusky glow. Cam hops off the boat to tie us off at the dock, then deposits my sopping wet clothes into a plastic bag and hands it to me, along with my now dry sandals. I slip them on, feeling silly in his big, oversized clothing and my strappy sandals, but grateful at the same time. I take his hand without hesitation as he helps me off the boat, silently enjoying the warm familiarity of his touch, and letting my mind wander back to the water, to the feel of his arms around me, my back up against his chest. It's my turn to smirk, now, a silly grin spreading across my face. Cam catches me, because *of course* he does.

"What are you smiling about?" he asks.

"Oh, you know. Just happy to be back on dry land."

We get into his truck and head back, both of us silent as the truck rumbles along down the twisting, turning back roads of Rocky Point. Even as darkness blankets the town, I know these roads like the back of my hand and anticipate every turn he makes. When we finally pull up outside of Tate Construction's office building, my car is the only car still in the lot. Cam pulls up next to it, puts the car in park, and quickly jumps out, coming around to open my door.

My heart flutters again at the gesture, a smile tugging at the corner of my lips.

"Well, thank you for an eventful evening," I say, unlocking my car and then turning to face him. He has that deadly serious look in his face again, and I feel my heart rate pick up.

He takes a step closer. "Sorry again for how it turned out."

His eyes are laser focused on my mouth, and I suddenly can't breathe. He takes another step toward me, his eyelids lowering, the tip of his tongue peeking out to wet his lips as his eyes search mine.

I should get in my car, shut the door, and drive back to Gran's as fast as I can. For some reason, though, my feet are glued into place and I can't peel my eyes away from the desire darkening Cam's eyes. I can tell he's waiting for some sort of sign that I want this, too, but I'm frozen. Mindlessly, I bite my bottom lip, and that's all the confirmation Cam needs.

Cam takes my face in his palms, the rough pads of his thumbs stroking my cheeks and sending shivers down my spine. I only look at him, wide-eyed as he lowers his head and presses his lips against mine, kissing me gently, as if he's still not quite sure where I stand. For a moment, neither am I, but the tension in his body tells me he's holding back, and, *damn it*, my brain is so scrambled. I let my eyes flutter closed, my lips parting, giving him permission to let go. With a growl, he deepens the kiss, his hands travelling to my hips and his tongue exploring my mouth while I let myself relax into him, my arms wrapping around his neck. I let myself get lost in Cam, the weight of the past pushing me toward him and melting away with every brush of his lips against mine. After what could have been a few moments or a few hours, he pulls away and untangles my arms from around his neck, his breathing ragged.

After he releases me, I sink back onto my car and press my fingers against my swollen lips, watching as Cam runs a hand through his hair and tries to catch his breath. Finally, he gives me a sheepish look, shoving his hands in his pockets and rocking back and forth on his heels. For a moment, he looks exactly like the eighteen-year-old boy I used to know.

"Well," he says. "Goodnight, Lizzie."

Laughing and shaking my head, which is still spinning from that amazing, dizzying kiss, I climb into my car and start it up.

"Goodnight, Cam."

Chapter Thirteen

Elizabeth

ROCKY POINT, MASSACHUSETTS

January 2010

"What the hell is that?"

Gran eyes me as I walk in through the front door, a zipped-up dress bag slung over my shoulder. Cam had *officially* asked me to go to Senior Prom with his last week, although I never really doubted we were going together. He's my boyfriend, after all, but it's still customary for the guy to do a "Promposal" and Cam did not disappoint. I met him in the gym after football practice on Friday afternoon, and had walked into the entire gym filled with flowers and Cam standing in the center, holding a sign that said: *Will you go to Prom with me?*

It was undoubtedly the best Promposal of the entire school, even better than how Dallas Adkins asked Ainsley Wells. I had secretly been excited to hear that Dallas' Promposal had actually been a little disappointing, although Ainsley had said yes. Now, I had the rest of the year and an amazing Senior Prom with Cam to look forward to.

"It's a prom dress," I say. "Cam asked me to go with him."

She scoffs, ripping the bag off my shoulder and unzipping it. The silky, dark azure fabric spills out of the bag, revealing the beaded Princess-cut neckline and long, full skirt. Gran roots around the bag, and my stomach sinks when I realize what she's looking for.

With a satisfied grunt, she pulls out the price tag.

Her eyes bulge out of her head when she sees the $300 tag, and I take a step back, worried about how she's going to react. Truthfully, the dress had been on sale. It was originally $500, but had been marked down because it was one of last years' styles.

"Where the hell did you get $300?" she asks, her tone as sharp as a knife. Defiantly, I grab the dress out of her hands and zip the bag buck up, holding it safely against my body.

"I've been picking up shifts at Java Point the last few months and tutoring after school. I saved up for it," I say, proud of myself that I was actually able to save up enough money to buy the dress on my own. I even had enough in my bank account that I could buy a used car if I wanted to, or put it toward books for college.

"And you decided to spend your hard-earned money on some ridiculous dress you'll only wear once? Stupid girl. I thought I taught you better than that."

Her words sting like a slap in the face.

"Gran, it's Senior Prom. Everyone goes, plus I got this dress on sale. I worked hard for it!"

"You worked hard, and you squandered the money away. Who does that remind you of?"

I swallow the lump in my throat, knowing she must be referring to my mother. Tears well up in my eyes but I refuse to let them spill. Why can't she just be proud of me? When will she realize I'm nothing like her? That all I want is to work hard and make something of myself? Why does she assume that I'm destined to fail?

"I'm going upstairs," I say, brushing past her and heading up the stairs toward the safety of my room. When I get to the stop of the landing, she calls up to me.

"If you're going to waste money or frivolous things, don't ever think about asking for my help," she sneers. "You're on your own."

"Whatever," I say, stomping into my room and slamming the door behind me. The force of it shakes the walls of my room, but I don't care. Laying the dress carefully down on my bed, I sit down and let the tears fall, knowing that no matter what, I'm going to have a great time at my Senior Prom.

When I finally calm down, I grab the picture of Cam and I off my nightstand and look at it, letting the memory take me back to a happier moment. Cam is in his football jersey, blue and gold paint streaks under his eyes and his hair a mess from his helmet. His arm is around me, pulling me in close to him, and we're both smiling without a care in the world. We took the photo right after Cam and the football team won the Thanksgiving game against our rival school, beating them out by a record number if points. I had been so proud to Cam's girlfriend in that moment. I still am, but I'm grateful, too. Whenever I feel like the world is crashing down around me, Cam is always there to lift me back up. There is always something to look forward to with Cam, whether it's getting milkshakes at the diner, or celebrating after game. Even Senior Prom.

As if on cue, my cell phone buzzes. I flip it open, and see that I have a text message from Cam.

Cam: How did dress shopping go? *kissy face*

Me: You'll have to wait and find out *winky face*

Cam: Oh yeah? You get something skimpy?

I roll my eyes. Cam has always had a dirty mind, but it's been worse ever since we had sex for the first time last summer. It had been both of our first times, which had made it really special, but ever since, Cam had been doubling down on the suggestive comments.

Me: Perv

Cam: *winky face* *kissy face* *tongue out face*

Me: Love you

Cam: Love you more

And just like that, I'm in my happy place again. In the cocoon of my bedroom, reveling in all the good times Cam and I have had together, and all the good times still to come, I let the hurt and anger from Gran and her perpetual disappointment in me wash away. Once we graduate, it will all be different. Once we graduate, Cam and I can do whatever we want, and I won't have to have Gran's insistence that I'm a failure hanging over me.

She doesn't want me to ask her for help? Fine. I won't have to.

I'm going to make something of myself, and I won't need anything from her ever again.

• • • •

PRESENT DAY

I let my hand hover over the doorknob, trying to find the courage to just turn it and step over the threshold.

Come on, Lizzie, it's just a bedroom.

Just a bedroom. A time capsule, more like. One that contains all the memories, good and bad, I left behind all those years ago. Of course, it's possible that when I left, Gran boxed everything up. It could be a shell of what I remember, containing nothing more than a bed and some furniture. Then again, I checked through all the boxes in both the basement and the attic, and none of them seemed to contain any of my childhood things. Maybe she just got rid of everything?

Only one way to find out.

Inhaling a shaky breath, I summon all of my courage and twist the doorknob, pushing open the door and stepping into my childhood bedroom.

Gran didn't get rid of anything. In fact, it looks as though this room hasn't been touched since I left for college ten years ago. My old bed is still covered in that purple polka-dot comforter I loved, and all the posters of my favorite bands and movie stars are still up on the walls, despite the corners curling in and the colors fading with time. My dresser, nightstands, and shelves are all still full of the knick-knacks I left behind, coated in a decades-worth of dust. I smile at the picture of Cam and I on the nightstand, from that record-breaking win against our rival school's football team, and pick it up, blowing the dust off. For a moment, I'm taken aback by how young and in love we look. I lift a finger to my lips, remembering the way he kissed me, and can't believe that was the same Cam that's in this picture.

It's been a few days since that kiss, and I'm honestly still reeling from it. I've kept myself busy, keeping gran company when Cheryl lets me know she's up and awake, meeting with her lawyer, and going through all the boxes in the basement and the attic. Gran asked me to figure out what all she had stored away, and has been slowly but surely giving me orders to throw things out, bring them to her apartment, or donate them, depending on the item. It hasn't been easy, but unearthing all these items from the past has been cathartic in a way. Somehow, it feels like together, Gran and I are giving ourselves closure over the things that happened so long ago, and finding a way to move forward. I've talked to her more in the last few weeks than I have in the last several years, and I'm starting to realize how precious the time we have left together really is.

A tear snakes its way from my eye down my cheek, landing on the dusty frame of the picture, and I collapse on the bed, my body wracked with guilt.

I left so much behind when I left Rocky Point, both good and bad things. Sure, I'd wanted to escape Gran's constant disapproval and show her I could make something of myself. But in the process, I'd lost the one thing that had gotten me through it all. I set the picture back down in its spot on the nightstand, then stand up and walk over to my closet.

I'd taken most of my clothes with me at the time, but a few things had stayed behind. Clothes that hadn't fit or that I no longer wore remained on hangers in the closet, as well as some shoes and handbags. Tucked away behind all of that, I catch sight of an opaque dress bag, zipped up tight.

My heart thuds in my chest as I realize what it is. I dig it out, bringing it over to the bed and gently setting it down. Carefully, I unzip the bag and spread it open, smiling as I take in the deep, dark blue fabric and shiny beaded details of my Senior Prom dress. Memories flood my brain of how much fun Cam and I'd had at prom, dancing the night away to our favorite songs and going out for milkshakes at the local diner afterward with friends. It had been a perfect night, and I'd felt like a princess.

Although, Gran *had* been right. I'd only worn the dress once.

Before I can unpack that thought, my phone buzzes in my back pocket and I take it out and look at the screen. My stomach twists into knots at the sight of my boss Whitney's name calling me.

"Hi, Whitney," I say, picking it up.

"Elizabeth, thank *God*," she says, emphasizing the last word. "I was starting to think you'd fallen off the face of the earth."

Fallen off the face of the earth? I've only been gone a few days.

"What do you mean?" I ask.

"Look, how quickly can you get back here? We just got a *huge* campaign, and it's going to be all hands on deck. We need you here," she says.

"Whitney, I'm so sorry. I thought I was clear that I would need some time off to deal with my Grandmother. I have a few weeks unused vacation time, remember?"

"Yes but that was *before* we landed this huge contract. You can't seriously expect to just leave us high and dry, Elizabeth. That's not what you're saying, right?"

Typical Whitney. Somehow, she is always able to make me feel guilty, or like I'm not being a "team player."

"Of course not, but..."

"Good," she says pointedly. "So, when will you be back?"

"I'm not sure," I say. "I still have quite a bit of loose ends to tie up here, I'm just not sure how long it will take."

"Look, Elizabeth, I like you. You're a go-getter and you're great at your job. But we need people on our team that we can rely on, and right now I'm having some doubts," she says, her tone dripping with forced disappointment. I swallow hard.

"You can rely on me, Whitney, I swear," I plead.

"Then I'll need to know when we can expect you back in the office, Elizabeth. And it can't be a few weeks from now. Otherwise, there might not be a job for you to come back to."

I close my eyes, inhaling a steadying breath. This can't be happening. I thought she said I could take my vacation time to sort everything out. Now what am I going to do?

But I need my job. I have a townhouse to pay for, and bills. Plus, who knows what Gran's situation will be. I can't afford to lose my job.

"Elizabeth?" Whitney asks impatiently. "Are you still there?"

"Yes, sorry," I say. "Look, give me a day or so to get things situated, and then I'll give you a definitive answer," I say hoping that's enough.

"And then you'll be back for good?"

Crap. "Yes," I say, thinking I'll just have to figure it out later.

"Fine," she says. "But I'll expect to hear from you tomorrow, Elizabeth."

"You will," I say. "Promise."

The line clicks, and I tuck my phone into my back pocket, my stomach in knots. I need more than one day to figure everything out. The house is still being worked on, and I haven't even talked to a realtor yet, but I'll have to figure it out.

The sound of an engine rumbling startles me, and I jog downstairs and look out the front window. Cam's black truck pulls into the driveway, followed by two large white vans with ladders on top and *Tate Construction* on the sides. I let out a shaky breath, my pulse quickening at the sight of Cam hopping out of his truck. I haven't seen him since he kissed me last night, and honestly, I'm not prepared to talk about. I haven't told anyone it happened, either. Not even Trisha, who will likely disown me for not calling her immediately after it happened. Squeezing my eyes shut tightly, I tell myself to calm down, then open them and step out onto the porch.

Cam's face lights up when he sees me, and my pulse goes into overdrive. *Is this what a heart attack feels like?*

"Hey there," he says, striding up to the porch and giving me a conspiratorial wink. Yep, we share a secret now. I give him a weak smile back, my nerves getting the better of me and the anxiety from my call with Whitney still hanging over me like a storm cloud.

"Hey yourself."

"So I've got some good news," Cam says. "Hank was able to wrangle up so extra help, and thinks we should be able to get the roof finished today *and* the inside re-drywalled. Plus, I heard back from my plumber friend and he thought it was just a pipe that needs patching, which he should be able to do tomorrow."

I let his words sink in. "Wow," I say. "So, all the work should be done by tomorrow?"

"Yep," he says. "You'll have to thank Hank, though. I don't know how he convinced everyone to come in on a Sunday. Probably offered them insane overtime, or something like that. I'll probably have to look into that, actually..."

"That's really great," I say, relief washing over me. If everything will be done by tomorrow, that means I can reach out to a realtor and have them list the property tomorrow, and get back to New York in time to save my job. I exhale a long, slow breath, Cam seemingly watching my every move. He quickly looks around at his crew, who are still unloading their trucks, grabs my hand, and then pulls me into the house. Once we're inside, he closes the door behind us and pulls me in close to him.

"Cam, what are you doing? I ask, laughing at how sneaky and secretive he's being. Then again, I guess we wouldn't want the whole world to know what happened between us last night.

"Let me take you to dinner," he says. "I still have to make up for the failed fishing trip yesterday, anyway."

Oh, I think he made up for it. "You really don't have to."

"I know," he says. "But I want to. How does tonight sound?"

I open my mouth to respond, but then close it again. Dinner would be a very public outing, and after last night, people would figure out that something happened between us. Is happening between us? *Crap.* I have no idea what to even think about what's going on between Cam and I now. We really need to figure that out. Plus, I need to come up with something to tell Whitney, and fast. I'll have to tell him I'm heading back to New York, just for a little while. I don't want him to freak out and think I'm just up and leaving him again. I just have to figure out this thing with work so that I don't lose my job, and I already still have so much to accomplish with the house and Gran.

Although... aren't I just up and leaving again? My life is in New York. When everything is said and done with Gran's house, there won't really be a reason for me to stick around Rocky Point for awfully long. Suddenly, a terrifying thought occurs to me. Does Cam expect me to stay in Rocky Point? Does he think that because of what happened last night, I'm going to be moving my life up here?

Oh God. Lizzie, you've really made a mess of things.

"Hello, earth to Lizzie," Cam says, giving me a concerned look. "Where did you go just now?"

"Nowhere," I say, shaking my head. "I'm good."

"So, dinner tonight?"

I have to tell him I'm going back to New York, and we *have* to talk about what happened last night. And I definitely can't let him take me out to dinner on a date. Not when I'm about to potentially hurt him, *again*.

"I don't know," I say. "I have a lot on my plate today. How about tomorrow?"

If I can buy myself just a little bit of time to sort everything out, then I can tell Cam my plans and make sure he doesn't misconstrue the situation. And maybe I'll have figured out my feelings by then, too.

"Tomorrow night it is," he says, grinning at me.

"And maybe we could keep it low-key," I say, thinking of how he might react to my news. Cam cocks on eyebrow, giving me a curious look. "So we could talk," I add. After a beat, Cam shrugs.

"I can live with that," he says.

"Great, I'll text you a little later today. I just have some errands to run first," I say, opening the front door and stepping outside. Cam follows me over to my car, looking around for his crew again. They are nowhere to be found, having walked around to the back of the house where they're setting up their ladders and equipment. Before I can get inside the car, Cam swoops down and kisses me, right in the middle of the driveway.

It catches me off guard, and for a moment I melt into his lips as they move over mine. Then, I remember we're in public and that anyone can be watching, and I swat him away.

"What?" he asks, winking and grinning at me.

"Someone is going to see!" I whisper, playfully pushing him out of the way. He shrugs, then blows me a kiss before walking toward the back of the house.

I'm in trouble, there's no denying that. And something tells me, leaving Rocky Point this time is going to be even more painful than last time.

• • • •

WHEN I STOP BY GRAN'S apartment later that day, she is in good spirits and seeming more like herself. Well, more lively, anyway. She hasn't said one nasty thing to me, hasn't given me a single mean look since I stepped inside, but rather has been joking and laughing with Cheryl and me. It's definitely out of character, at least for her to not be the least bit repulsed by my presence, but I'll take it. For the first time in my recent memory, being with Gran feels... *normal*. I brought over some old photographs and yearbooks I found from when Gran was in high school, and I thought it might be fun to look through them while Gran is feeling well. When I show her the yearbook, she takes it from me and runs her small, wrinkled hands over the leatherbound cover, the year 1947 embossed in shiny, gold numbers against the dark blue leather.

Gingerly, Gran flips through the pages of the yearbook, her eyes awash in memories from her own childhood. Every now and then, she stops to show Cheryl and I a picture, or regale us with a story of she and her friends raised hell and almost got caught. It's a side of Gran I've never seen. She never talked much about her past when I was growing up.

She pauses on a full-page, black and white picture of a boy in a football uniform, helmet in one arm, the other arm around a pretty, somehow familiar girl in a ruffled peasant dress, her hair done up in pin curls and a wide smile on her face. She traces her finger over the picture, a small sigh escaping her lips. Curious, I look over at Cheryl, who shrugs and mouths, *no idea.*

"He was so handsome," Gran sighs, turning smiling but tearful eyes toward me. Alarmed, I scoot in closer to her.

"Who was?" I ask.

Gran smiles, a tear escaping down her cheek. "Your grandfather."

Cheryl gasps across from me, practically falling out of her chair, and I can feel my mouth drop open, my palms going clammy in shock. My grandfather? Never once has Gran ever mentioned my grandfather, other than to tell me he died before I was born. Growing up, Gran hardly talked about anything from the past besides drilling into me all the mistakes my mother made. I'd always been curious, both about my parents *and* Gran's late husband, but I never dared to ask. I always figured it would upset her, and I put a lot of effort into avoiding upsetting Gran most of the time. To think of this man that way, *my grandfather...* it was odd, yet somehow comforting at the same time.

But that must mean... "Gran, is that you in this photo?"

She returns her damp gaze to the picture. "Yes. That's me and Henry Quinn, your grandfather, and the love of my life."

The words hit like a punch to the gut, and I can feel tears welling up in my eyes. I look over at Cheryl, who is dabbing at her eyes with the sleeve of her sweater, and then back to Gran, who is smiling wider than I've ever seen her before.

"Joseph was a good man," she says. "We were high school sweethearts, and we got engaged shortly after we graduated high school, a few weeks after this photograph was taken. We were married not long after that."

"Gran," I say, reaching out and placing my hand in hers. She wraps her frail fingers around mine and squeezes. "I had no idea," I say, truly in shock.

"I know," she sighs, shaking her head. "I never told you about your grandfather when you were young. The memories were still too painful. But it's not right that you know so little about your family, and I'm so…" her voice cracks, and she looks at me, tears streaming down her face. "I'm so sorry for that, Elizabeth."

I feel a stray tear escape from my eye and travel down my cheek. Never in a million years could I have imagined I'd have this moment with my grandmother.

"It's okay, Gran," I say, sniffling and patting her hand. "No need to be sorry."

"It took me years to get pregnant," she continues, looking between Cheryl and I as she recounts a story no one has likely heard for decades. "We were married ten whole years before I got pregnant with your mother, and when I did, we were both so thrilled. It was a dream come true, really. When your mother was born, both of us thought it was the happiest moment of our lives, bringing this little, precious bundle into the world. It wasn't long after your mother was born, though, that Henry developed his cough. It was a horrendous cough, the kind that wracked his entire body. Sometimes, he'd be up all night just coughing and coughing…"

Gran looks out into the distance, remembering. I squeeze her hand tighter.

She continues, "When he finally went to the doctor, it turned out to be lung cancer. They said there was nothing they could do; it had grown too big. He was gone within the year."

Silence falls over the room, as Cheryl and I exchange pained glances. Gran's husband had died of lung cancer not even a year after they'd had their first, and *only*, child? Suddenly, all of the pieces are clicking together in my head, a million tiny lightbulbs going off, one by one. Gran had had a baby, and lost the love of her life, practically all at the same time. She must have been terrified, raising an infant all by herself, and feeling an unimaginable amount of grief. Then to think of what happened to my mother, what became of Gran's only daughter...

I swallow hard, the lump in throat growing harder to swallow.

Gran turns to me again, her hand swiping at the tears on her face. Surprisingly, she raises a hand to my face, and cups my chin.

"You remind me so much of that time, Elizabeth. You, and that boy, Cam. You're just like Henry and I were. Young, and in love."

I freeze, her words sending a chill down my spine. Cam and I? I shake my head, realizing she must not remember that it's been ten years since Cam and I broke up. That, or she thought that we were still together, somehow, when she saw him the other day.

"No, Gran, Cam and I aren't together anymore. That was a long time ago, and I'm not sure if we can ever get back to that. Time is just not on our side."

Her eyes crinkle, a mixture of mirth and sadness shining through in her smile.

"Oh, Elizabeth. If there's one thing I've realized recently, it's that time is the most precious thing we have. And *love* never wastes it."

Chapter Fourteen

"WELL, YOU CERTAINLY have a spring in your step today."

I look up to see my mom walking up my driveway, a tray with two coffees from Java Point in her hand and Bella at her heels. I set down the shovel I was using to dig out a space for a flowerbed in the front yard of my house, and go over to greet her, wrapping one arm around her in a hug.

"I could say the same about you," I say. "Thanks for the coffee"

She walks over to where I've been digging and assess the plot, nodding her head in approval.

"Are you going to plant the impatiens like I suggested?" mom asks, inspecting the space.

"That's the plan," I say. Mom has always had a green thumb, something that I inherited. She was super excited when I told her I'd be planting some flower beds around the house while I worked on the landscaping.

We each take a sip of our coffees, mom narrowing her eyes at me. She gives me that *mom* look, that *I know you did something, and you better tell me what* kind of look.

"Something wrong?" I ask. I have a feeling I know what this is about, but I'm not going to offer it up. Nope, if she's going to snoop and meddle, then she'll have to own it. She'll have to ask me herself.

"Nothing's wrong," she says, taking another sip of her coffee. "I've been hearing a *lot* of chatter from the town gossips though, that's for sure."

"Is that so,' I reply, more of a statement than a question.

"Mhm," she says, watching me like a hawk. I'm not going to give her the satisfaction of giving it away. I set down my coffee and pick the shovel back up, continuing to dig. Mom huffs at me impatiently. "The salon in town has been buzzing with a story about a particular local contractor reuniting with a long, lost love."

I turn to face her, one hand on my hip and the other balancing on the shovel.

"Spit it out, mom," I say.

"Well, I heard from Betty that Maeve Waller was driving past Tate Construction a few nights ago and thought she you and Elizabeth getting *very* cozy together, if you know what I mean."

My heart rate shoots into overdrive at the mention of Elizabeth and the other night, and I have to bite my cheeks to keep a smile from spreading across my face. I didn't know what had possessed me to think I could kiss her, but I was even more surprised when she kissed me *back*. And it hadn't just been some chaste, gentle kiss. No, it had been hot, and needy, and everything I could have hoped it would be. Hell, I had to take a cold shower when I got home just to calm down. I could barely sleep the last few nights, replaying it in my head over and over again.

"Betty didn't believe it, of course," my mom continues. "That is, until she happened to be in the neighborhood of Helen's house this morning and saw it for herself!"

I lower my eyes to the ground. *Crap.* Someone saw us? I probably should have been a little more discreet when I kissed her in Helen's driveway, but I couldn't help myself. I'd been thinking of the feel of her soft, perfect lips on mine since she'd driven away last night. I didn't think anyone had been watching.

"Do you have a point you're trying to make?" I ask, but it backfires, because she just gives me another one of her infamous *mom* looks that practically compels me to spill the beans. I give her a heavy sigh, then nod my head. "Okay," I say. "I kissed Lizzie, so what?"

My mom beams at me, clapping her hands in front of her. "I knew you'd find your way back to one another," she says.

"Mom, stop, it's not like that," I say. "It was probably a one-time thing, anyway."

"Well it sounds like it was a two-time thing," she says, wiggling her eyebrows. I cringe.

"Okay, a two-time thing then. Seriously, don't make it more than it is."

I mean it, too. As much as I enjoyed our kiss, and frankly, as much as I'd love to do a lot more than kiss her, I have to take it slow. I know that Lizzie is only in town to get Helen situated, and to fix up the house. She's not staying for the long-term. At least, not yet. Maybe, though, with some time, I can convince her that Rocky Point is where she belongs. Rocky Point, *and* with me.

The minute she kissed me back, I knew that there would be nobody else in the world like Elizabeth Quinn. I have never been able to find something even remotely close to what Lizzie and I had, and if anything, that kiss had just confirmed for me that all those years of being angry and hurt, all that time I spent devoting every ounce of energy into my business so that I could forget the pain of her leaving, it had all been for one thing: to make me into the person I need to be for her. Eighteen-year-old me didn't have any direction or ambition. When Lizzie left for college, I was bitter, and angry, and selfish. I wanted to be the center of her world, and that would have only held her back. Now though, I see that we both grew up to become exactly who we needed to be. And as much as it kills me to think that my mom, and Gray, and Eddie were right, I have to believe that this is our second chance.

I still need to ease Lizzie into it, though. She has a lot going on with Helen's illness and all the painful memories being back in Rocky Point must be digging up. I don't want to scare her off, or move too fast. I need to be careful, and I need to convince her that I've changed, that I'm the type of man she deserves now. And to do that, I *might* need a little help.

"Do you think you can help me get the flowers in before this evening?" I ask my mom, who rolls her eyes and pulls a pair of gardening gloves out of her pockets. She gives me a knowing look.

"Sure I can, but may I ask, what's the rush?"

"I just might want to show the house off soon," I say, evading the intent I know was behind her question. "And I would really love it if the house looked nice."

"Uh huh," she says, slipping on her gardening gloves and pointing toward the porch, where several flats of color, barely blooming impatiens, and other colorful annuals. "Those the flowers?"

"Yep, I'll finish digging out this bed if you want to start bringing some flats down. I've got mulch in the back."

"You got it." She gives me a thumbs-up and starts walking toward the porch, Bella following closely behind her.

"Thanks, mom!" I call after her. She turns around and gives me a conspiratorial wink.

"Anything for my favorite son!"

• • • •

LIZZIE DID SAY SHE wanted to do something low-key, so I've devised the *perfect* plan. I'm going to cook her dinner in my beautiful new kitchen, and show off all the work I've put into my house so she can see exactly what sort of man I've turned into. Plus, a little bit of privacy might be exactly what I need to convince her that there's a life for her here in Rocky Point.

After finishing up planting in the flower beds, which went much faster than anticipated thanks to my mom's help, I head into town to the grocery store to grab ingredients and supplies to make Lizzie the perfect dinner. *Hopefully.* I'm more of a take-out or microwave dinner kind of guy, and to be honest I really don't cook all that much. But I'm going to go with steaks, because I'm pretty sure I should be able to nail that. Plus, pair it with a nice bottle of red wine, and there's no way I could go wrong.

I'm not *really* a wine drinker either, so I had planned to just grab whatever looked good. Now, standing in front of the millions of options for red wine, I realize what a rookie mistake I made in thinking I could just grab a bottle and go. Grabbing two bottles off the shelf in front of me, I stare at the labels and try to figure out the difference between a Malbec and a Cabernet. Is there even really a difference? Is red even the best wine to go with steak? I thought I heard that somewhere. *Shit*.

"I'm more of a Riesling girl, myself, but if I had to pick between those two, I'd go with the Malbec over the Cab."

I straighten, the familiar voice an unwelcome and unexpected sound, like nails on a chalkboard. I don't have to turn around to know that Ainsley is behind me. I also don't need to turn around to know that she's striking her signature pose: arms crossed, one hip cocked out to the side, her lips pursed, and her nose crinkled, like she just smelled something gross. It's the same pose she used to strike in school whenever she was being a typical popular girl, and it's *also* the same way she stood when I told her I thought we should break up. Like I said, signature pose.

Since the last thing I want is to think about Ainsley while I'm having dinner with Lizzie, I put the Malbec back on the shelf and decide to go with the Cabernet and drop it into my cart.

"Well, I hope she's a dry wine kind of girl," Ainsley continues. Not in the mood for her antics, I turn to face her, doing my best to keep a straight face when I see she is indeed standing exactly like I thought she would be, a shopping basket hung over her arm. I let out a long, exasperated sigh.

"What do you want, Ainsley?"

"Oh, nothing," she says innocently. "Just saw you browsing the wines and thought you must be planning a pretty big night. Since I've never seen you drink anything other than beer, I figured you could use a second opinion."

"I'm doing just fine on my own, thanks," I say, and she rolls her eyes.

"Oh, I've heard all about how well you're doing. It's all anyone can talk about at the salon. You know how people *love* to gossip," she says. She takes a few steps toward me, a sly smile spreading across her face as she adds, "I heard you took her out on the boat. Remember when you took me out on the boat?"

I inhale sharply. Of course I do, although I don't remember actually getting out onto the water. In fact, I distinctly remember wanting to take Ainsley out on the boat, as I'd just recently gotten it, but the moment she set foot on the deck, it became pretty clear she had things other than sailing in mind. She'd dragged me into the small cabin and... well, that had been the extent of our boat trip.

I clear my throat. "I don't see how that's relevant."

Without asking, she reaches into my cart and picks up the pack of steaks, and raises her eyebrows. "Wow, you're cooking for her? I don't even think I knew that you *could* cook."

"Look, Ains, it's really none of your business."

She flicks me a sharp, dagger-like look and puts the steaks back into the cart. "Calm down, Cam, I have no interest in you cooking for me. I do, however, feel that as your friend, I have an obligation to be honest with you."

"Oh, we're friends now?" I ask. Considering how she laid into me at Ryan's the other night, in front of the *entire bar*, I never would have thought she considered me a friend.

Ainsley shrugs. "I just think you should be careful, is all," she says. "I would hate to see you get your heart broken *again* by Elizabeth Quinn."

"Well, thanks for your concern, but it's really not necessary," I say, trying to push past her. In typical Ainsley fashion, she stands in front of me, not letting me pass. Knowing Ainsley, I'll need to wait until she's said her peace before I can go on with my life. I put my hands up in surrender. "Okay, okay. I'm listening."

She crosses her arms over her chest, smirking victoriously. "Elizabeth left once, Cam. There's nothing stopping her from leaving again. I just think you shouldn't expect too much, or you're going to get hurt."

"Trust me, I'm not expecting anything," I say.

"You say that, but I *know* how devastated you were when she left the first time. And I know you think she can do no wrong, but she's selfish. She did what was best for her then, and she'll do it again, with or without you."

Ouch. Okay, as unfairly as I may have treated Ainsley in the past, she's really swinging below the belt.

"Like I said, I appreciate your concern, but it's really none of your business," I say, hoping she gets the message that I am done with this conversation. She cocks an eyebrow, as if to say, *message received.*

"Fine," she says sharply. "Just don't come running to me when she's gone and you're in that dark place all over again." She puts a hand on her hip and turns dramatically on her heel, marching away from the wine aisle. I wait until she is out of eyesight before I let myself exhale.

I try to shake off Ainsley's negativity while I purchase the items in my cart and head back to the house, but when I pull into the driveway, I realize there's suddenly a nagging feeling in the pit of my stomach that wasn't there before. Ainsley's words had planted a seed of doubt within me, and every intrusive thought about whether I could do it, whether I could eventually convince Lizzie to stay, watered that seed until it grew into knotted, twisted vines that messed with my head, and my confidence.

I know that I've got my work cut out for me if I'm going to convince Lizzie to stay in Rocky Point, but I'm up for the challenge. I let her get away once, and I won't make the same mistake again. Screw the past, screw the gossip, and screw Ainsley's negativity, I'm going to make it happen.

Chapter Fifteen

Elizabeth

ANY UPDATE?

I'd gotten the text message from Whitney first thing in the morning, and wanted desperately to blow it off. Truthfully, work was the least of my worries, not with everything going on. I texted her back that I still needed more time, but she didn't respond. I figured it was for the best. Gran's doctor had done a CAT scan, and determined the deterioration in her brain was progressing faster than expected. We could expect continued confusion and disorientation, and further memory loss, most likely eventually leading to a diagnosis of Alzheimer's Disease. The news had been a blow to both Cheryl and I, who had both rushed over to Golden Acre's at the doctor's request only to be met with the bad news. He'd sent me on my way with a packet of papers and pamphlets, suggesting I educate myself the best I could on what to expect of Gran's condition in the coming months.

Still not wanting to face the inevitability that I would lose Gran from my life almost as quickly as I'd gotten her back, I find it nearly impossible to read through the treatment options. Then again, I've been stuck in the kitchen for so long, first talking with the plumber, then going over paperwork with the lawyer, and now this, that I wonder if I just need a change of scenery. I move to the attic, thinking I can just mindlessly sift through boxes and bins for a little while, and give my brain a break. Two hours later, though, I've only made it through one box and somehow feel even more exhausted than when I started.

My cell phone buzzes, indicating that I've received a text message, and my heart sinks. It's probably Whitney, finally firing me because she's had enough of my indecision. I pull it out and inhale a deep breath, but then freeze when I see the name across the screen.

It's from Cam.

My heart rate picking up, I open the message.

Cam: We still on for tonight?

A smile tugs at the corner of my mouth. With everything going on, I had forgotten about Cam's invitation for dinner tonight. The thought is both anxiety-inducing and exciting, because I could definitely use the break and the company, but something tells me it won't just be a dinner between friends.

Me: Absolutely

I hit send before I have too much time to think about it or chicken out. My phone buzzes almost immediately after, Cam's name popping up on the screen again

Cam: My house. 7:30.

I reread the text a few times, my heart thumping in my chest. A text with his address follows, and I pop it into the GPS app on my phone to see how far away it is, and am relieved to see that it's only a few minutes away. That means I still have plenty of time to get ready, select and outfit, and give myself a pep talk so I don't head screaming for the hills.

I pull up to the address Cam sent me right at 7:30, and let out an awe-filled sigh as I take in the house before me. Like most of the houses in Rocky Point, it's a traditional Cape with cream-colored siding and freshly painted maroon shutters, a matching maroon door sitting front and center. The high pitch of the roof is covered in new, dark gray shingles, a tall, red brick chimney sticking out from the right side. The driveway, smooth and glossy from recently laid asphalt, extends up to an attached two-car garage, inside which I can spot Cam's pick-up truck. Off of the driveway, large slate rocks form a whimsical path through the manicured, dark green grass, lined with tulips of every color and leading up to the front porch. The porch itself is framed by flower beds that extend all the way around to the side of the house, and a swing hangs by two thick, metal chains from the wide gabled roof, covered in a plush maroon cushion. It's strange to picture Cam owning a house, especially one that looks like it's been plucked right out of a fairy tale. It makes me curious as to how the inside looks.

I step out of the car and make my way up the winding rock path, admiring the bright pops of color from the tulips and the myriad of impatiens surrounding the house. When I step onto the porch, the maroon front door opens and Cam appears, the sight of him taking my breath away even more than the house.

His usual casual t-shirt has been replaced by a tailored black collared shirt, the first few buttons undone and the bottom of the shirt untucked. He's clean shaven, which I haven't seen since coming back to Rocky Point, just a hint of a five o'clock shadow visible on his chiseled jawline. He leans against the doorframe, hands in his pockets, looking somehow relaxed and like a damn cover model at the same time. It's a whole new Cam, one I've never seen before, not even when we were kids. Cam, the GQ model. And I have to admit, I'm *digging it*.

Lord, have mercy. I haven't even stepped inside yet and I'm already swooning.

He takes his dear, sweet time raking his eyes from the thin straps of my yellow sundress that falls a good few inches above my knee, down to the cream-colored ribbon ties of my espadrille wedge heels, and back up again. My cheeks heat under the scrutiny, my heart racing as a thin smile tugs at the corner of his mouth. His gaze lingers for a moment on my hair, which is pulled into a loose chignon at the nape of my neck, then locks onto mine with an intensity that knocks the wind out of me.

"Your house is beautiful," I say, desperate to fill the silence between us. My mouth has gone completely dry, and I inadvertently wet my lips. His eyes, dark and heavy, dart to my mouth, settling there for a moment as if he's deciding whether to invite me in or haul me over his shoulder like a damn cave man. I can see the set in his jaw, the flick of his pulse in his neck, and the heat in my cheeks blossoms across my neck, chest, shoulders, until my entire body feels like it's on fire. I catch sight of a garden hose out of the corner of my eye and figure, at least if I burst into flames, someone will be able to easily put me out.

"Do you want to come in?" Cam asks, stepping aside holding open the door. I nod my head, my brain apparently deciding we've lost the ability to speak, and step past him into the foyer.

My scrambled brain is momentarily distracted by how absolutely beautiful the interior of Cam's house is. The hardwood floors, which look to be original but restored, carry through the entire first floor and give the little house a ton of character. I peek around, each room revealing a beautiful, surprising detail restored from when the house was originally built. In the living room, there's the wide, brick gas fireplace that's been carefully rebuilt with a large wooden beam added as a mantle. In the kitchen, a vintage copper vent hood has been cleaned and polished, lending a bit of rustic charm to the otherwise modern space. A small sitting room off the back of the house showcases a large, built-in bookshelf that's been updated and painted white. Everything, every single little detail, is immaculate and charming. I can't believe this is Cam's house.

"Did you do all the renovations?" I ask, certain he must have. He's a contractor, after all, so he certainly has the skill and the resources. He just nods quietly.

"Every inch," he says, doing his best to appear humble.

"Wow," I say, as we return to the kitchen and take a seat at table. Cam pulls down a few wine glasses and uncorks a bottle of red wine, pouring me a generous glass. Without hesitation, I take a large sip of the wine and pray that it helps calm my nerves.

"So, I wanted to cook you dinner," he says, taking a sip from his glass too. "But it turns out I'm a pretty terrible cook."

I laugh, shaking my head. "I doubt that," I say, and then realize I don't actually smell anything cooking. "What are you making?" I ask.

"Well, I had *planned* on steaks," he says, casting his eyes to the ground. "But it turns out once they catch fire, they're pretty unsalvageable."

"No!"

"*Yes*. By the time I was done with them, they were a pile of ash. I had to air the house out for at least half an hour before you got here."

"Oh no," I giggle, taking another sip of the wine. I can already feel the liquid warmth from the Cabernet going to work, loosening up my otherwise tense nerves. "Well, I'm not picky. We could always just do takeout."

"I'm glad you say that. I already have the finest lo mein and pork fried rice from China Garden on its way as we speak."

"As long as you also ordered egg rolls," I say, polishing off my glass and holding it out for a refill. "Those are my favorite."

"I know, and don't worry. I ordered some of those, too," he says, topping both of our glasses off.

If I don't slow down on the wine, I'll be useless here in a few minutes. But at least for now, the magic properties of a good, full-bodied red wine are doing their job and helping me to continue to form sentences instead of clamming up and implode, so I guess I'll have to pick my poison.

"How's your mom?" I blurt out, in a pretty crappy attempt to make conversation. *Right, because that's not an awkward question at all.* God, Lizzie. Get it together.

"She's good," he says, seemingly unaffected by the rapid change in subject. "She's been keeping herself busy with her little dog, Bella. I swear, she treats that thing better than she ever treated Grayson and I."

I perk up at the mention of Grayson's name. "How is he doing?"

"Well, he's moved on from breaking tourists' hearts in Rocky Point to breaking the public's heart in Hollywood. He landed a part on *While the Globe Spins*."

My jaw practically hits the floor. "No way! I used to watch that show all the time. Until they brought on that newer actress. The young one, long black hair, leggy. What's her name?"

"Ariana Lopez," Cam says.

"Yes! That's it. She's terrible," I say.

"Well, Grayson is apparently dating her. Although, he says it's not serious."

"Stop it, you're kidding!" I say, practically jumping out of my seat. "He's practically famous, then!"

"Yeah, don't let him hear you say that. It'll go straight to his big head, and we definitely don't need that."

• • • •

A FEW HOURS LATER, we've killed the wine and our take-out Chinese food, and are laughing over the memory of me going overboard on Cam's boat.

"I was pretty sure you were going to get eaten by a shark or something, and then Trisha would murder me for being reckless and taking you out there," he says, draining the last few sips of wine from his glass.

"Oh, so it's Trisha's wrath you're worried about, not mine?"

"Have you seen her get mad?" he asks. "I'd rather get eaten by the shark myself. She may be bubbly, but she's got a temper. I don't know how Eddie does it."

"Fair point," I say, a sudden thought coming to me. "You know, I do have a question, though."

"What's that?"

"Why *Sid's Sea Maiden?*"

Cam laughs at the mention of his boat's unusual name, nodding his head.

"The boat's previous owner, Sid Sutton, named it that. I haven't got the balls to change it," he explains. I cock my head to the side, not sure what he means by that.

"Can't you just... pick a new name?" I ask, and his face grows serious.

"Oh no," he says, leaning both his elbows on the table. "Naming a boat is very serious business. Renaming a boat? Even more serious."

"Come on," I say, polishing off my glass too. "How serious could it be?"

"First, you have to remove every single item or instance of the original name from the boat and destroy them. I mean everything, paperwork, knick-knacks, any captain's logs, maintenance records, it's all got to go," he says.

"Okay, I mean, that doesn't seem *that* bad..." I say, but he holds up a hand.

"Once you've destroyed all evidence of the former name, you have to appease the Gods of the sea. Poseidon, or Neptune, or whatever. You have to recite a call to the Gods and ask them to keep the boat safe from harm. Then you have to pour a whole bottle of Champagne into the water, from East to West."

"You're kidding," I say, but he keeps going.

"After that, you have to address all four winds. Individually. North, South, East, and West. And you have to ask them for good winds and fair weather."

"Let me guess," I say. "You have to pour out Champagne for each of them, too?"

"You got it," he says. After you address each wind individually, you pour out some champagne in that specific direction."

"That's very involved."

"Exactly," Cam says. "And I don't feel like messing with fate, so, *Sid's Sea Maiden* it is."

"If you were going to rename it though, do you know what you would change it to?" I ask.

Cam looks toward the ceiling, deep in thought. "I guess I never really thought about it," he says.

"I mean, you could go cliché," I say. "Like *The Odyssey* or *The Black Pearl*. Or punny, like *Seas the Day*."

"I think I'd want something more original than that," he says. "Something more... romantic? That's why *Sid's Sea Maiden* is such a good name. It evokes a sense of adventure, and long-lost love. It's classic."

"I think that wine is going to your head," I tell him.

"Maybe," he concedes. "Maybe one day, I'll be inspired enough by someone to change the boat's name."

He looks at me then, his eyes dark and serious, and I swallow hard, suddenly feeling very sober. I push out my chair and stand up, walking my wine glass over to the sink. It's late, and since I slacked off today, I'll have to work twice as fast tomorrow. I'll need to get some sleep if I have any hopes of making it through Gran's boxes anytime soon.

"Well, I should be..."

I turn around, and Cam is up and in front of me, his body mere inches from mine. I let out a small gasp at the closeness, the intoxicating smell of his cologne or aftershave enveloping me, making me want to move in just a little bit closer.

"Cam," I say, exhaling a shaky breath. "I don't... I can't..."

"What's wrong?" he asks.

"I'm just... scared. I'm scared of how you make me feel. I'm scared of how easy it is to be with you."

"I'm scared too, Lizzie," Cam breathes. "I never thought I'd get to see you again, let alone spend as much time with you as I have these last few weeks. It's like my life has been on hold this whole time, just... waiting for something. Waiting for you."

I raise my eyes to meet his, biting back the tears suddenly threatening to spill over. The truth is, I feel that way, too. Like I've just been in a holding pattern, circling, waiting for the moment when life would start again. I don't know when exactly it happened, but coming back to Rocky Point, to Cam, it's like the fog has lifted and I've finally been given the all-clear to be myself again.

He looks down at my arm, where the strap of my dress has fallen off my shoulder, and takes the thin yellow fabric in between his thumb and his finger, rolling it around for a moment before dropping it back where he found it. Rather than remove his hand, though, he trails a finger up my arm and onto my shoulder, letting it sit where the strap should be for just a moment before tracing a line across my collarbone, the feeling of his rough skin sending shivers of desire over every inch of my body. His hand comes to my heart, and he rests his palm there, letting his hand rise and fall with the suddenly ragged heaves of my breathing. He glances at me, his gaze hot and full of wanting, and in a flash the air between us is electrified. Then, with his other hand, he tips my chin up toward him, his mouth claiming mine in one swift, sudden movement.

For a moment I stiffen, letting out a squeal of surprise, before melting into his embrace and his kiss. I let him in, parting my lips and allowing him to explore and taste and devour every inch of my mouth. My hands twist in the fabric of his shirt, pulling him in closer, feeling more terrified and more free than I have since leaving Rocky Point so long ago. Back then, I was running away. Now, it feels like I'm coming home.

Releasing my mouth, Cam rests his forehead against mine, giving us both a moment to catch our breath. His hand trails down my arm, to my waist, pulling me flush against him.

"I want this so bad, Lizzie. I want *you* so bad. More than I've ever wanted anything in my life."

Moving from my waist, his hand trails down my thigh, slipping under the hem of my dress until it meets bare skin again. I gasp, both startled at his touch and desperately wanting more as he gently trails his hand up my thigh, little by little, planting kisses along my jaw until he reaches my ear and nips at my earlobe.

"What do you want, Lizzie?" he asks, his breath on my neck sending a wave of tingles across the delicate skin. I shiver, turning my head up toward him until his lips are on mine again. He gives me another deep, passionate kiss, before pulling away again.

"Cam," I breathe, my voice throaty and urgent and I reach for him again, but he holds me in place.

"I need to know what you want, Lizzie. I need you to tell me," he says, his tone gentle but firm. His eyes search mine, full of wanting and desire despite his restraint. I swallow hard, my hand findings its way to his face, cupping his cheek in my palm.

"I want *this*, Cam. I want *you*."

Without wasting another moment, his lips find mine again, kissing me even more hungrily than before. My arms weave around his neck, my fingers threading through his hair, my body needing to be closer to his, as close as possible. His hand continues its path up my thigh, eliciting a gasp as his thumb brushes gently across the thin fabric of my underwear, my entire body quivering under his touch. He teases me with his thumb, his mouth never leaving mine, until I am shaking and breathless in his arms, the whole world slipping away around us. He moves his hand from my thigh, despite my small moan of protest, and grinds into me, his arousal pressing against me even through his jeans.

"Christ, Lizzie," he breathes, his chest heaving, but I'm done with going slow. I'm done thinking, deciding. My fear is gone, replaced with the need to be with Cam, to remember what it feels like to touch him and taste him and be with him again. I drop my hands to the waistband of his jeans, my fingers clumsily fumbling with the button until it finally pops free. Before I can slip my hand underneath his waistband, though, he grabs my wrists and holds them still.

"Please, Cam," I say, but he shakes his head.

"Not here," he growls, gently pulling me by the wrist and leading me toward the stairs. I follow, the air around us growing more and more electrified as he leads me down the hallway, and into the bedroom.

Chapter Sixteen

Elizabeth

THE FEELING OF A LARGE, strong arm pulling me in closer stirs me awake, my brain taking a second to catch up and remember where I am. I stay as still as possible, my legs tangled between Cam's and the sheets, my back pressed snugly against the warm, firm expanse of chest. I take a moment and listen to the gentle sound of his breathing, feeling the slight rise and fall of his chest, memories of the night before flooding me. Memories of Cam's lips on mine, of his hands on my body, of the way all those years of heartache, and anger, and needing each other clashed in an unforgettable night of passion.

Reaching for my phone on the nightstand, I pause when I feel Cam stirring beside me. I don't want to wake him, but I can see light streaming in through the tall, floor-to-ceiling window, and we went to sleep so late, I have no idea what time it is. When he settles back into that soft, snoring rhythm again, I quickly grab my phone and check the time.

I groan internally, knowing I need to get back to Gran's and get back to work, but not wanting to move from the comfy, warm cocoon of Cam's embrace. Sighing, I remove Cam's arm from around my waist and climb out of bed, eliciting a grunt of protest from Cam, whose eyes flutter open. He watches with sleepy, sexy eyes as I slip on my clothes from the night before, fixing my messy, just-rolled-out-of-bed hair into a knot at the top of my head.

"I think you should definitely come back to bed," Cam mumbles, rubbing his eyes and sitting up. I chuckle, sitting on the edge of the bed to slip on my shoes.

"As nice as that sounds, I have a *lot* to get done today. I'm way behind."

"I'll come help," he says. "I can even bring coffee, in case you need a bribe of some kind."

"Don't you have, like, a company to run?" I ask, standing up and putting my hands on my hips. He gives me a lazy smile, and my heart skips a beat.

"Hank can hold down the fort for a little while."

"Well, alright then."

I lean down and give him a kiss on the cheek, and his hand cups my chin, holding me still while his lips find mine. I sigh into him, not wanting to go, but knowing if I don't bite the bullet and go, I'll be another day behind in my to-do list.

"Skinny Vanilla Latte, please," I say, earning an eye roll from Cam. "Extra espresso."

"You got it."

• • • •

CAM FINDS ME IN MY childhood bedroom about an hour later, two big coffee cups in his hand, his hair still slightly damp from a shower.

"The barista at Java Point looked terrified when I asked for extra espresso. Apparently, there's already two shots in this size," he says, handing over the coffee and watching with amusement as I take a long drag from it. I close my eyes and smile, savoring the warmth of the beverage as the caffeine starts to work its magic.

"Just give me a few minutes to let that enter my bloodstream, and I'll be human again in no time."

"Okay, coffee fiend. I think we might need to stage an intervention."

Cam walks slowly around the room, his eyes darting around at all of the memories preserved like a time capsule on the shelves and walls. He picks up and inspects a few items – a bronze medal from a debate competition in ninth grade, the blue and gold tassel from my graduation cap, a polaroid from Senior Prom. I watch as he scans the picture, grinning before placing it back in its place on top of my dresser.

"I can't believe this room looks exactly the same as it did back then," he says, turning to face me. He points to the polka-dot bedspread and wiggles his eyebrows. "Even your bed looks just like it did when we... ya know..."

"Okay, yes, it does," I say, interrupting his eyebrow wiggling with a playful jab to the shoulder. "I'm trying to figure out what to do with all this stuff. Most of it I haven't thought of in years, but I can't bring myself to throw any of it away."

"I mean, you should definitely keep the bedspread," he says, winking at me. "Good memories."

"If the memories mean so much to you, I guess you can just have it," I offer, playfully winking back at him.

"I might take you up on that," he says. I scrunch my face in disgust, shaking my head.

"Yuck, okay. Let's move on."

My cell phone rings in my pocket, and I pull it out absentmindedly, my heart thumping in my chest when I read the name on the screen.

Whitney.

Damn it. I totally forgot to call her yesterday like I was supposed to. By now, she's probably out for blood if she hasn't decided to fire me already.

"I'm sorry, I have to take this," I say, and Cam nods.

"No worries, I'll just be here checking out what other memories you have lying around," he says, wiggling his eyebrows again. I respond with a dramatic eye roll, before stepping out into the hallway and answering the phone.

"Hi, Whitney," I say, feigning as much enthusiasm as I can muster. There is a short pause on the other end of the line before Whitney responds.

"Elizabeth, so good to hear from you. I worried when I didn't hear from you that perhaps you were ill, or that something had happened. It's wonderful to know you're perfectly fine."

I hold my breath, letting her sardonic tone roll off. I *did* promise to give her an update yesterday, and I'd completely forgotten. She's completely within her right to be peeved.

"Whitney, I'm so sorry I didn't call you yesterday. Things have just been..." I hesitate. Busy, getting wrapped up in Cam when I'm supposed to be taking care of my grandmother and then getting back home? "Crazy," I say, settling on something a little less specific.

"I'm sure," she says, drawing out the last word. "So, now that we've established you're not sick or missing, when can we expect back you in the office?"

Whitney's question is pointed and direct, and meant to convey that she's not messing around. She wants an answer, and she wants it now. Trying to think of the right thing to say, I squeeze my eyes shut and weigh my options. On the one hand, I still have responsibilities in New York, and I can't exactly afford to lose my job. On the other... I have a lot of unfinished business in Rocky Point, too. Whitney's patience with me has clearly run dry, though, and that means I'm left with really only one option.

"Right away." My voice is shaky as the words reluctantly come out. "In fact, I'm leaving tonight, right after I tie up the last few loose ends here."

Another pause on the other end of the line sends my heart practically jumping into my throat.

"Excellent. We'll expect you first thing tomorrow, then," she says after a beat.

I swallow hard. "You can count on me."

The other end of the line drops, and I let out a long slow breath, massaging my temples and trying to calm my heart that feels like it's about to beat out of my chest. I'm not ready to leave Rocky Point yet. The roof on the house is fixed and the plumbing issue has been taken care of, but I still need to let the realtor know I'm ready to list it. There's still so much to go through in Gran's house, so much uncertainty around her health, that leaving feels... irresponsible somehow. And then, as if all of that wasn't reason enough to stay... there's Cam.

I can feel my heart breaking in my chest as the realization of what this means for Cam and I sets in. The timing couldn't be worse. It seems like we literally just found our way back to each other, finally let ourselves explore what could be between us. And now, almost as if the universe is trying to play some cruel joke on me, it's all going to get ripped away. If I go back to New York, I can't promise how long I'll have to stay, or when I'll be able to come back to Rocky Point. If I can't get more time off, I'll be stuck. I'm not even sure that weekends will be a possibility, not if this new project is as big as Whitney says it is. When Whitney says *all hands on deck*, that usually means we're working around the clock until it's finished. I used to be okay with that. Actually... I used to thrive on that. On the pressure, and the chaos, and the thrill of driving myself and my team so hard that we were winning awards, and all-expenses-paid vacations to tropical resorts.

There was another side to all of that, though. Long nights where we barely slept, subsisting on nothing until the wee hours of the night just to hit a deadline. Going out to the bar after a long week with coworkers and completely overdoing it, just because it helped us to forget about the stress for a little while. Sometimes, you'd work so hard on an ad campaign just to have it pulled at the last minute, because the client reconsidered or picked someone else's. Whitney would always say it's about balance, that the good things about the job always make up for the bad. But lately, it had started feeling like there were less and less good days, and I've been starting to get burnt out. I'd thought coming to Rocky Point would only be added stress, but instead, it gave me perspective on the things that are truly important. Things like family, and friendships that aren't built over competition and alcohol. Things like love.

Love. I loved Cam once. And if the last few days have shown me anything, I could probably love Cam again. It would be so, so easy to fall for him just like I did when I was a teenager. Even though we've grown and changed over the years we've been apart, we managed to pick up right where we left off. And maybe I don't know what the future holds, or if the feelings between Cam and I are real, but it seems unfair to both of us not to give it a chance. Gran's sad but sobering words replay over and over again in my head: *time is the most precious thing we have.* I've already wasted enough time, being angry at Gran and being apart from Cam. It's about time I made up for all of it.

I spin around, ready to march back into my childhood bedroom and tell Cam that I'm ready to try, ready to put the past behind us and move forward. I want to explain that I'm going back to New York for a few days but somehow, I don't know how yet, but somehow, I'm going to figure out a way to be in Rocky Point for good. Maybe it's crazy, and maybe I haven't thought the logistics all the way through, but it feels *right*, and I know that I have to follow my head and my heart.

When I turn around, Cam is already in the doorway. His tall, broad frame practically takes up the whole thing, the light from the bedroom casting an eerie silhouette of his outline. His arms are crossed over his chest, his mouth a thin, tight line. He looks... angry.

I take a few steps toward him, but he puts up a hand to stop me.

"You're leaving," he says. It's not a question, but rather a matter-of-fact statement. I open my mouth to respond, but close it again, realizing he must have overheard my conversation with Whitney on the phone.

I shake my head, trying to organize my thoughts.

"No... well... Cam, if you'd just listen..."

"You're leaving *tonight*," he says, stressing the word. *Tonight*. I had told Whitney I'd be leaving tonight, and that I'd be back in the office first thing in the morning. But that's what I *had* to say, to keep her from firing me on the spot. If he would just let me explain.

"Okay, yes," I say, finding it hard to look Cam in the eye when there's so much anger behind his gaze. "But it's not what you think..."

"No," he says, shaking his head. "It's exactly what I think. You're leaving, *tonight*, and you weren't going to tell me. You were just going to disappear back to New York, *again*, just like you did ten years ago."

A lump forms in the back of my throat, his words cutting through me like a knife. It's the last part of what he says that really hurts. *Like I did ten years ago.* As if this is the same situation, as if I'm the same person I was back then. Can't he see that this is not the same thing at all?

"Cam, if you just let me explain," I plead, my voice cracking, tears beginning to well up in my eyes. "I don't have a choice. I have to go back, but..."

"You have a choice. Just like you had a choice back then. And your decision is loud and clear, Lizzie."

He brushes past me, barreling down the stairs. I follow after him, but I can hardly keep up with his long legs, taking the steps two at a time. He stops at the front door, bracing himself the door with one hand, his head hung low.

"Cam, just *wait*," I say. "Please."

He turns around to face me slowly, his eyes glassy.

"I'm done waiting, Lizzie. You need to go back to New York, so go. But I'm done waiting. I've been living in an endless cycle of regret and anger, thinking I let you get away, beating myself up for not fighting for you back then. I was so determined not to make the same mistake this time, not when life had given me a second chance. But now I understand, no matter how hard I fight, it's not going to be enough. It's never going to be enough. You're always going to leave."

"Cam, that's unfair," I say, the dams breaking and tears streaming down my face. I don't know how to make him understand. "I don't want to go, but I have to. I was going to tell you, but..."

"Just like you were going to tell me last time? After you'd already made the decision? After last night I thought..." he pauses, shaking his head. "It doesn't matter, because I clearly thought wrong."

"You're not even giving me a chance to explain," I plead, but he swings open the front door and steps onto the porch.

"I don't want you to explain, Lizzie. I don't want your excuses. You needed your Gran's roof fixed, and you got it. You needed a break from your life, and you got it. As far as I'm concerned, my work here is done."

He slams the door behind him, the entire house shaking with the force of it, including me. I stand, frozen on the bottom of landing of the stairs, listening to the rumble of his truck as he starts it up and peels out of the driveway. It takes me a few moments for my breathing to return to normal, and when it does, the realization hits me like ten tons of bricks.

Cam is gone, and he's not coming back. And if I don't pack up my things and get back to New York, my life there is gone, too.

Chapter Seventeen

Cameron

A LOUD BANGING AT MY door startles me into consciousness, and I almost fall off the couch in my living room. I catch myself before I hit the floor and sit up, rubbing my eyes and looking around. The room is dark – all the curtains are drawn tightly shut – but the little halo of light peeking around them tells me it's still daytime. I stand up and almost trip over an empty bottle of beer laying on the floor, rubbing the crick in my neck. It feels like I slept on a cinderblock.

The banging continues, the loud sound reverberating uncomfortably against my skull, and I walk carefully to the door, trying to avoid the rest of the debris and clutter on the floor.

Okay, so I haven't been taking Lizzie's leaving well. At all.

It's been a few weeks, and at first, I was angry. So angry, that I just did everything I could to distract myself. I worked nonstop, and put the energy into making sure we turned around contracts that rolled in as fast as we possibly could. I rode the guys hard, until Hank told me I was acting like a total asshole. I eased up, tried to get myself back to normal, but that's when the anger started to replace itself with that familiar sense of guilt and regret.

Should I have tried to be more understanding? When I overheard her telling her boss that she'd be leaving that night, I'd been overwhelmed by the sense of betrayal I'd felt when I realized history was repeating itself. Lizzie was leaving again, and I had no say in the matter. Not that I should have expected to have any say this time around – it's not like we were together or anything. But I would have at least thought, after the night we'd shared together, she would have the decent to give me a heads up. Anything other than letting me hear it secondhand, *again.* She had tried to explain, but I didn't want to hear it. I'd left, and she'd gone back to New York, and I felt like a miserable prick.

I had retreated into my house and a few cases of beer, drowning out my sorrows while I came to terms with the fact that I'm a fucking idiot. My mom had tried to call me at least a hundred times, and I'd ignored them all. I didn't want her to worry, but I couldn't face her yet, either. I wasn't ready for a lecture on how I overreacted, how I should have listened to her, tried to work it out. I'm still not.

The banging on my door continues, the sound actually making me want to punch a wall. "Hold your damn horses, I'm coming!" I yell, peeking through the small window in the door and seeing Hank on my front porch. He's got bags under his eyes the size and color of 8-balls, and if I didn't already feel like the worst Goddamn boss in the world, I do now.

Hank gives me a once over when I open the door, his eyebrows shooting up as he takes me in. I'm fairly sure I look like shit, but I honestly haven't looked in a mirror in days.

"You look like hell," Hank says, confirming my suspicions.

"Thank you?"

"I just came to check on you, man. Been a couple of days since I've heard from you, we're all starting to get a little worried," Hank says, shoving his hands in his pockets.

I clear my throat, turning my head toward my bare feet. "I'm doing fine, Hank."

"Like hell you are," he says, rolling his eyes. Typical Hank, calling me out on my bullshit. When I don't respond, he adds, "Well are you going to invite me inside, or what?"

With a long sigh, I take a step back and hold open the door for him to come inside. Squinting into the darkness, he looks around and scrunches his face up.

"What the hell is that smell?" he asks.

"I don't know what you're talking about," I say, and he shakes his head.

"When's the last time you showered, Cam?"

I think on it for a moment, but apparently, I take way too long to respond.

"Never mind," Hank says, shaking his head. "I don't even want to know."

He walks through the house, flipping on all the lights as he goes, mumbling his disapproval at the mess in each room. Sheepishly, I follow him into the living room, where I've spent the majority of the last few days. Hank throws open the curtains and turns around to observe the mess, disgust written all over his face.

"Christ, Cameron," he says, gripping the back of his neck. "All this over a girl?"

My hand comes to my temples, a headache brewing. I'm not really in the mood for Hank's judgement, but I suppose it's warranted.

"Well Hank, you've seen me, I'm still alive. Is there anything else you need or can I go back to wallowing in peace?"

"Is there anything else I need? Yeah, Cam, I need my boss back. *We* need our boss back. We're busy, bro. You spent two weeks riding us like a hard-ass and then disappeared off the face of the earth. I've been trying to pick up the slack where I can, but I'm only one person. I can't be in ten places at once. Shit's starting to slip, man. The guys are tired. I'm tired."

My eyes widen as Hank lays into me, a side of the guy I definitely haven't seen before. I grip the back of my neck, feeling a wave of embarrassment come over me, but I don't really know what to say.

"I'm sorry, Hank. I didn't realize it was that bad."

"Look man, I know you're hurting, but I'm starting to worry. I've never seen you like this before, and the guys are starting to talk. Everyone's wondering if you've gone off the deep end, and they're a little freaked out for their jobs. I don't blame them, either."

Shit. I didn't mean for this. I didn't mean for Hank or any of the guys to feel scared for their job. Hell, they're the *lifeblood* of Tate Construction. Without them, the whole thing falls apart. They're good guys, they don't deserve this. They deserve a boss who has his act together, or at least one that's not actively flushing his life down the toilet.

"You're right, Hank," I say after a beat. "I've been a crappy boss, I'm sorry. Look, let me jump in the shower and I'll meet you at the office."

"Good, you smell like death," he says, cracking the slightest smile.

"And tell the guys we're having an all-staff meeting in an hour. I want to clear a few things up."

Hank nods. "You got it, boss."

I show him out and take a quick shower, trying to wash away the shame and embarrassment from Hank seeing me like that. He's absolutely right, I need to get my shit together. Hopefully, though, I can put my guys' minds at ease and move past this once and for all.

• • • •

HALF AN HOUR LATER, I pull up to the office freshly showered and clean shaven, feeling a little more like myself. As had become my routine when I *did* leave the house, I took a detour by Helen Quinn's house on my way. I'm not sure why it had become my habit; maybe a part of me was hoping to find Lizzie there, back in Rocky Point for good. Maybe, I needed to see that the For Sale sign that had gone up a few weeks ago was still there, to know that all those memories weren't yet gone forever. Something about seeing that sign, still standing on the lawn, kept the tiniest flicker of hope alive within me.

Kylie eyes me palely as I enter the lobby, her usual sunny demeanor looking like a shadow has been cast over it. She stands abruptly, her tell, slender figure rigid and tense.

"Mr. Tate," she says, the forced pleasantness in her voice edged with concern. "I wasn't expecting you today. How are you feeling?"

I give her a weak smile, feeling guilty that my misery has permeated not just my foreman and my crew, but Kylie, as well. "I'm good, Kylie. Thanks for asking."

"Before you go to your office," she says, her eyes saucer-like, a hint of panic shining through. "I... um, well... your mother stopped by."

"My mother?"

Kylie nods her head so fast, that I worry it might snap right off. "Yes, your mother. I told her you weren't in, that I didn't think you'd be in at all today, but she insisted on staying. She seems..."

"What?" I ask, my heart rate picking up. Why would my mother camp out in my office when I'm not even at work?

"Upset."

"Did she say why?"

"No, Mr. Tate. I'm sorry, I should've asked, but was she distraught, and..."

Distraught? "It's okay, Kylie. Thanks for letting me know," I say trying to be as calm as possible. Kylie exhales a shaky breath, returning to her chair, her back its usual ramrod straight.

"Of course, sir."

Deciding I better leave Kylie to calm down, I head down the hallway to my office where the door is ajar, light spilling out into the hallway. I peek my head inside to find my mother sitting at my desk, her slim frame engulfed in the plush executive office chair, her nose deep into a magazine. I clear my throat, drawing her eyes up from the magazine for a brief moment, and eliciting a dissatisfied sigh that lets me know my mother is *very* upset with me.

"Mom, what are you doing in my office?" I ask, keeping my tone as upbeat as possible. She sets the magazine down and folds her hands in front of her, and I realize for the first time that she should have been a cop, or a judge, or something. The way she looks in that chair, coupled with the narrowed eyes of her *you're in trouble* stare, she could get anyone to confess to anything.

"Oh, just wondering when my eldest son was planning to return to civilization," she says pointedly. I notice I'm the *eldest* son today, and not the *favorite* son.

"Sorry, mom. I know I've been a little... off the grid lately."

"If by 'off the grid' you mean sulking in your house in your underwear. Don't think I didn't realize you were screening my calls."

She's not wrong. "Sorry," I say, feeling more and more like a boy whose mother is getting ready to put him in time-out.

"I'm sure you are. But you're the *least* of my worries," she stands up, one hand on her hip, the other pressed against her forehead. She begins to pace the small office. "You sabotage your own happiness, sure. But at least you're not ruining your career. I mean, you and I *will* talk about Elizabeth, that's not a question. But Grayson..." she sits back down, leaning her chin into her hand. "I wish your father were here. He'd know how to deal with you boys."

Grayson? I roll my eyes and slump down into the chair opposite her, leaning my elbows on my knees. I could have sworn I told her *not* to read the tabloids, and what did she do? She read the tabloids.

"Mom, what did I tell you about the tabloids?" I ask, my turn to play the stern parental figure. She just narrows her eyes at me.

"Well, Gray doesn't answer his phone, and you've been avoiding me for the last few weeks, so what else was I supposed to do to make sure my baby boy is doing alright? After what I've been reading, though, I wish I hadn't picked it up at all!"

As much as it kills me, it *does* pique my interest.

"Okay, I'll bite. What are they saying about Gray now?"

It only takes about .7 seconds for her features to soften, and for her to flip open an article in the magazine with a picture of Gray and Ariana Lopez, their faces inside a clip-art broken heart. She slides it toward me and points, looking stricken.

"This article is *slandering* your brother, that's what," she says. "They're making up stories that he broke up with his co-star for some model, Olivia-something. Can you believe that?"

Olivia-something? A model? "Olivia Knight? The supermodel?" I ask, and to my surprise, she nods. "Are you kidding?"

"No, it says it right *here*," she insists, jabbing her finger at the page. "But that's not even the worst part!"

"And that is?"

"That tramp Ariana Lopez is refusing to work with him! She's trying to get him fired from the show!"

I close my eyes and let out a long, slow breath. "They're always making stuff up, mom. Don't believe everything you read."

"But what if it's true? What if she *does* get him fired?"

"Have you even talked to Gray? I bet none of it's even true."

"He won't answer the phone or call me back," she says. "I just hate seeing this stuff and knowing he's so far away. I can't talk any sense into him."

"Look, I know Gray's the baby of the family, but he is a grown man. He can make his own choices, *and* his own mistakes. You have to give him some space, mom."

"Oh, I know that," she says, wrapping her arms around herself. "I just worry, is all. About *both* of you."

"I know you do," I say, reaching over and giving her arm a squeeze.

"*Which* reminds me," she says, pointing a finger in my direction. "We have some things to talk about."

Mom gets up and walks around to my side of the desk, leaning against it and crossing her arms over her chest. She eyes me knowingly, waiting, as if she's giving me the opportunity to speak before she launches into her lecture. Figuring it won't make a difference either way, I just lean back in my chair and hold out my hand, signaling for her to go ahead and lay it on me.

"Well," she starts, "I guess we should talk about why you've been sulking the last few weeks."

I snort a laugh. "Do we have to?"

"Yes, we do. Tell me how you left things with Elizabeth."

Rolling my eyes, I shift uncomfortably in my chair. Considering everyone has been talking about how Lizzie and I left things, I seriously doubt I need to enlighten my mother.

"Don't you already know?" I ask.

"I want to hear it from you."

Sighing, I grip the back of my neck and nod. "She was going to leave again without telling me. She let me believe we had a chance to make things just like they used to be, and then without any warning at all, she was going to leave. I didn't think I could go through that a second time."

Not that it had been any easier, me being the one to leave. If anything, it had just felt... wrong, like I was leaving a piece of myself behind. Like I was giving up.

"So, you're doing just fine with all this, then?" my mom asks, one eyebrow cocked. I narrow my eyes at her.

"Fine with this? How could I possibly be fine with this? I have loved Lizzie Quinn since I was fifteen! Of *course* I didn't want her to go, and of course I wish we'd left things a little differently." I stand up, my heart pumping so hard I can feel my pulse in my ears, and begin pacing the room. Does she really think I'm *fine*? I screwed up, and I know it. Except this time, I didn't even ask her to choose. I chose for her. And the last few days, I've been wondering if I chose wrong. "She tried to explain, but I didn't want to listen. I know she probably had a good reason, even if I didn't let her tell it to me. And now, she's gone, and there's nothing I can do about it. I had a second chance at happiness with Lizzie, and I blew it."

I raise a guilty gaze to my mom, who's wearing a victorious look on her face, her lips pursed, a smirk tugging at the corner of her mouth.

"Have you told her any of that?" she asks.

"I... what? No," I say, to which mom responds with a shrug. She walks over to me and gives my arm a squeeze, before heading for the door. Before she leaves, she turns around to give me one last nugget of motherly advice.

"Sometimes, we have to fight hard for what we want, Cameron. Love might be a risk, but it's always one worth taking."

Chapter Seventeen

Elizabeth

When I walk back into my condo in New York and flip on the lights, I realize for the first time that the space looks... *sterile.* Everything is some shade of white or light gray, with clean, geometric lines and all surfaces free of any trace of clutter or knick-knacks or really *anything* that might make it feel more like a home. I look around in awe as the thought comes over me that this place is not cozy, or warm, or inviting, or any of the things that a home should feel like. Even the view, an enviable and classic New York skyline which at one time I would have killed over, seems to only widen the space around me. I'm like a planet, drifting out in the universe, my closest neighbor lightyears away. I'm isolated, and alone.

At one time, that what all I wanted. To just be *alone.*

Back then, alone didn't feel lonely. Alone merely felt like a bi-product of crushing my goals, of doing what I set out to do: make something out of myself that would prove everyone wrong. And I did that, ten times over, in fact. So why, standing in the bare, character-less entryway of my highly sought-after condo in the middle of the most popular city in the country, do I suddenly feel like a failure?

Love.

I have none of it.

I spent so much time working on turning myself into something or someone that I believed to be worthy, that I completely neglected to build any lasting relationships in my life. Like somehow, I just forgot to make memories that weren't job promotions or working overtime. I never had the chance to know my parents, and now, I might have missed out on the chance to have a relationship with my last surviving relative. I never allowed myself to be distracted by romantic relationships, and after seeing Cam again, I'm starting to realize that I very well may have lost out on life's most important gift.

I take a step into my bedroom, and sigh at the same sterile, white atmosphere. When did my bedroom, the room that used to be my *sanctuary*, start to look more like a hotel room than the place I should have safest, and comfiest, and most at home? The plush, starched-white bedspread that used to feel like some sort of cloud now just makes me think about the night I spent in Cam's bed, warm and most certainly not alone.

I've known what to do the moment I got in my car and left Rocky Point, but now that I'm here, looking at the remnants of ten years of a life on hold, I can't wait any longer. I'm not willing to waste any more time.

Picking up the phone, I frantically dial Trisha.

• • • •

"TRISHA, I DON'T THINK I can thank you enough," I gush, gripping my phone so tightly it might just slip out of my clammy hand any moment. "I never would have thought of this myself, and it's perfect."

"Any time!" Trisha practically yells into the phone. I have to pull away from it for a moment, her voice is so loud. "I'm just happy that you'll be back in Rocky Point, I was starting to like having someone to hang out with other than my husband."

"Me too," I say, genuinely excited at what the future holds. I gave Whitney my notice the other day, and am planning to move back to Rocky Point to be able to be closer to Gran. Whitney was... furious, to put it lightly. She told me I was screwing over her and the team, and that I was selfish and clearly did not care about my career. I let it roll off; it only confirmed that I'm making the right decision leaving New York and going back home to Rocky Point. Plus, Trisha has helped me to figure out what I'm going to do for work when I get there, and I couldn't be more excited.

I am going into business for myself as a freelance advertising and marketing consultant, and Dearing Hardware is going to be my first customer. Trisha seems to think that the town and the myriad of small businesses that make it up could benefit from someone who could manage their advertising and marketing. I didn't think it would work, but Trisha showed me several businesses in town that are willing to sign year-long contracts, and is sure more will be interested once they see what I can do. She even set up a call between myself and the town's mayor to discuss how my services could be used to advertise and market the town to drive tourism during the summer. With Trisha's help, I'm confident that I'll be able to get my own business up and running in no time.

I took Gran's house off the market, and listed my condo in New York, instead. I've gotten several interested buyers in just the few days it's been listed, and my listing agent is fairly sure it will sell within a few weeks. As scary as it's been to uproot my entire life as I know it, strike out on my own in my career, and confront the past moving back to Rocky Point, it's also been exciting, and just feels *right*. It helps to have a friend as great as Trisha in my corner, too.

"All that's left to do is to pack up your things and make it official," Trisha says. "Have you told your Gran yet?"

I had called Gran to tell her. At first, she hadn't really understood why I would want to do such a thing. When I explained to her how important it was for me to be closer to her, to spend as much time as I could with her, she had both surprised and a little weepy. I had been, too. We might not have been as close as we could have been throughout the years, but I'm not planning on wasting anymore time. We'll make the most of the time we have left, before Gran's illness gets in our way.

"She was very excited," I say, and I can hear Trisha squeal on the other end of the line. I roll my bottom lip between my teeth and bite down, a question I've been debating on asking ready to leap impatiently off the tip of my tongue.

"I can hear the steam coming out of your ears from here," Trisha says. "What's on your mind?"

"How... um..." I clear my throat, which has suddenly gone drier than the desert. "How's Cam? Have you heard from him?"

There's a long pause on Trisha's end of the line.

"Eddie says he hasn't really been himself, whatever that means," she says. "Apparently Hank's been sending in any orders to the store, which Eddie thought was odd. And the handful of times Eddie's gone over to deliver materials to the office, Cam hasn't been there. One day, Eddie asked that redheaded supermodel Cam's got behind the front desk if she'd seen him, and she said Cam hadn't been in in about a week."

My jaw hangs slack as Trisha speaks. I hear what she's saying, but I just can't believe it. That business isn't just Cam's livelihood, it's his *life*. And he just suddenly stopped showing up?

"Maybe Cam's just busy. Or maybe he took a vacation or something," Trisha adds, sensing my concern. If he took a vacation, why wouldn't Kylie just say that?

I've thought a lot about the way Cam and I left things, and I can't help but feel guilty, like everything that happened was all my fault. I should have told him what was going on with work, that my boss was pressuring me to leave. I should have been honest with him before we'd gotten so close. I let him believe we had a chance at something, and then did the one thing that would be sure to cause him pain: left Rocky Point, and him, for New York without any warning. And to top it all off, I didn't even tell him. He had to overhear it.

If he had just let me explain before he'd stormed off, I could have told him about my plans to come back. Granted, I didn't have all the details worked out then, but I knew I wanted to try. I can't help but feel like I should have stopped him, tried harder to explain, done *something* to stop him from thinking I was running away again. I wanted to pick up the phone and call him so many times, but I just didn't know what to say to make it right. And I know I'll have to confront Cam eventually, when I'm back in Rocky Point full time. I doubt we'll be able to go back to anything like what we might have had, but I'll have to try. Maybe, if he doesn't hate me so much, we can at least be friends.

"Maybe. I just hope I haven't completely ruined things."

I hang up the phone and peer around at my townhouse, mountains of empty boxes stacked against the walls, waiting to be filled with all the things and memories I've accumulated since college. The sad part is that more likely than not, it's all going to end up in storage. I'll always treasure the time I spent in New York, but the more I plan my move, the more I realize what I need is a clean slate. A *true* fresh start, in my relationship with Gran, in growing my friendship with Trisha, and in building my career in Rocky Point. And maybe, just maybe, I'll get a fresh start with Cam, too.

Chapter Eighteen

Cameron

IT'S GONE.

The For Sale sign in Helen Quinn's yard, the one I've driven by every day for the last month, is no longer there. I saw it this morning, on my way to a job site, but on my way home... just, gone.

It took most of the drive for it to really hit me. After driving by Helen's, I spent the rest of the ride home in silence, my brain totally blank and running on autopilot, trying to come to terms with what that missing sign really means. Twenty minutes later, I still can't seem to get out of my truck, even though I've been parked in front of my house with the engine off and my stomach is growling.

If the For Sale sign came down, then Helen's house sold. If Helen's house sold, then... it's over. Lizzie has no reason to come back to Rocky Point, at least not for more than a few days. All of her ties with Rocky Point have been successfully and completely severed. Ultimately, I knew this was the most likely outcome, but a part of me had fought against accepting it. Because accepting it would mean admitting that I'm out of time, and admitting that I'm out of team would mean...

Well, it would mean that I blew it.

I did blow it. Bad.

Headlights pulling into my driveway beside me pull me out of my momentary self-loathing, and I slide out of my truck with a sigh. Stuffing my hands into my pockets, I watch as my mom climbs out of her SUV, scoops Bella into her arms, and walks toward me. I'm not expecting her, but she has an uncanny spidey-sense for whenever one of her sons is going through a crisis, or ruining their life. It's annoying.

"I wasn't expecting you, mom," I say, stuffing my hands into my pockets. "Everything alright?"

"Oh, I just came to see if you'd heard the news," she says, giving me a sympathetic smile and lightly patting Bella's head. "I figured you might need to... talk."

See? All I had to do was spend half an hour sulking, and her psychic mom abilities kicked in.

"Yeah, I heard the news alright," I huff, turning around and walking toward the house. I can hear mom set Bella down, the dogs' collar jingling as they follow closely at my heels. "And I don't want to talk about it."

Mom and Bella follow me into the kitchen, where I pour myself a glass of water and chug it down in one go. I'm hoping she'll get the message, but her obstinate stance and narrowed gaze tells me otherwise.

"You're not really taking it how I thought you would," my mom says, placing her hands on her hips.

How did she think I would take it? Should I be jumping up and down and throwing confetti? If anything, I'm amazed I grabbed a glass of water before the bourbon I keep stashed in my pantry.

"Well, I'm not sure how you think I should be reacting," I say, filling up the water glass again and downing it. "It's not like I didn't see it coming."

Mom's eyebrows draw together, her face going from incredulous to downright confused. "What do you mean? You expected this?" she asks.

"Well it was only a matter of time before she sold the house. That was always the plan. And I'm sure as shit not happy about it, but what can I do?" I say, and I'm completely, totally surprised when my mom bursts out laughing.

"Sold the house?" she asks, in between giggles and laughter-induced hiccups. "Oh, Cameron."

"What?" I ask, my annoyance growing by the second. "What is so damn funny?"

Mom walks up to me and puts a hand on my shoulder, her face softening. "She didn't sell the house, sweetie. She took it off the market. She's moving back."

For a moment, the whole world goes fuzzy, fading to black as my brain digests the words I just heard. I blink a few times, the kitchen and my mom's sympathetic face coming back in to focus, my hands gripping the counter behind me so that I don't topple over. My mouth feels like sandpaper, even though I just chugged two full glasses of water. *Did she say Lizzie is moving back?*

"What are you talking about?" I ask, the words more of a croak than a full sentence.

"I heard Elizabeth sold her place in New York, quit her job, and is moving back to Rocky Point. Sally Rittenhouse, you know her and her husband own that little sandwich shop down by the marina? Well she was telling me that Trisha Dearing reached out to them, told them Lizzie Quinn is going to be working as an advertising consultant in town, and asked if they'd be interested in having her do all their ads. They're really excited to hire her on," mom explains. "And they aren't the only ones. Apparently, she's already got a ton of eager clients."

I lean down and plant a kiss on my mom's cheek, then bolt toward the front door. She runs after me, Bella growling and chasing behind her.

"Where are you going?" she calls after me, as I burst through the front door and onto the driveway.

"Eddie's!" I yell back, climbing into the cab of my truck. Mom comes around to the drivers' side and knocks on the window, which I impatiently roll down.

"Why are you going to Eddie's?" she asks.

Because I need to talk to Trisha.

Because I need to figure out exactly when Lizzie is coming back to town.

Because somehow, by some miracle, I'm getting another chance. And this time, I'm not going to mess it up.

"I have something to take care of," I say, and with that, I put the truck in reverse and gun it out of the driveway, leaving my mom standing there looking surprised, and Bella yapping at me as I tear off down the street.

Chapter Nineteen

"JUST SAY YOU'RE COMING!" Trisha pleads, and I roll my eyes, sighing loudly enough that I hope she'll hear me. I've only been back in Rocky Point for a few days, but I've been consumed with my new business, and sorting through all my stuff to figure out what needs unpacked, and what needs to be put into storage. Trisha's been trying to help where she can, but she doesn't have *that* much free time, what with working at the hardware store and all. Since coming back to town, interest in my new advertising consulting venture has doubled since Trisha initially provided me a list of leads. Apparently, business owners around town, and even some in neighboring towns, are extremely excited about the idea of not having to do their own advertising. Some are even willing to pay extra, if I'll help them do a rebranding. All this work means I'll be replacing my full-time income in no time, but at the same time, I'm going to be *very* busy. And in the midst of it all, Trisha wants me to meet her at the marina for dinner. "*Pleeeeease!*" she adds, using her best guilt-inducing voice.

"Trisha, I'm sorry, I'm really busy," I say, guilty to disappoint her but knowing there's no way I could possibly step out right now. "I want to hang with you, I do, but if I don't get myself organized, I'll be setting myself up for failure."

"Come on, it's *just* a few hours," Trisha whines, a hint of her former drama-queen-self shining through. "I'll come over first thing tomorrow morning to help out. Besides, I *did* help you land these gigs in the first place. Think of it as a 'thank you.'"

Boy, she's really laying it on thick. I squeeze my eyes shut, feeling my willpower crumble despite my efforts to remain on task. Would a few hours really kill me? Probably not. Besides, I'm bound to have a late night anyway, considering how nervous I am that none of this is actually going to work out. I didn't sleep last night. Not sure what would make tonight any different. And on that note, I suppose I *can* spare a few hours to go to dinner with my friend who helped make my new job a reality in the first place.

"Okay," I say, having to pull the phone away from my head at Trisha's squeal of delight, or risk bursting my eardrum. When she settles down, I ask, "Where do you want me to meet you?"

"The marina," she says, her voice suddenly conspiratorial. "Five o'clock *sharp*, got it?"

"Got it."

Another squeal on the other end of the line reverberates my brain before the line goes silent, and a momentary wave of panic overtakes me. It's the height of the summer season, which means the marina will be packed. I'm sure I'll run into all kinds of people who will want to confirm the town gossip, ask me about Gran and my new business, and try to get the latest scoop. According to Trisha, my little fling with Cam was all anyone could talk about after I left, and I'm not sure I'm ready to face questions about that yet. Even worse, I'm not ready to face Cam yet. What if we run into him? I'm half tempted to call Trisha back and tell her to forget it, but I know she'll be disappointed, and I can't do that to her.

Hoping to distract myself, I decide the best thing to do for the next few hours is bury myself in my work, and not let thoughts of tonight, or of Cam, creep back into my mind.

Easier said than done.

• • • •

THE EARLY SUMMER HEAT and gorgeous views always draw people to the shops and plentiful outdoor dining of the Rocky Point harbor, and when I arrive at five o'clock, the harbor is packed with people milling about. I'm met with nods and smiles as I make my way through to the marina, making me feel a little less on edge, considering I've been terrified of who I might run into all day. I find Trisha standing by docks, looking out over the water, her face lighting up when she sees me coming.

"You made it!" she exclaims, throwing her arms around me in a hug. Then, she grabs my hand and starts pulling me toward the docks. "Come on, we have to hurry."

"I thought you said we were going to dinner," I say, my suspicion growing as we head toward the neat lines of powerboats, fishing boats, and small yachts that take up residence on the marina docks. Trisha looks back over her shoulder and winks, before yanking me along, and my stomach begins to twist into knots.

"Just follow me!" she insists, tightening her grip on my clammy, sweaty palm. I do as I'm told, the knot in my stomach growing larger and larger with every twist and turn we take until she stops abruptly in front of a familiar center console fishing boat, a devilish grin on her face.

"Trisha, what's going on?" I ask, my heart rate speeding up, my heart thumping so hard I can feel it beating in my ears. Trisha finally releases my hand, her features softening as she looks toward the boat. "Trisha," I demand, my breathing nervous and raggedy now. "Why in the world are we standing in front of..."

"Lizzie."

He says my name softly, his voice tinged with a hint of surprise, as if he doesn't fully expect me to be here. I turn toward the voice, my eyes taking in the sight of Cam on the deck of his boat, his eyes wide and full of determination as they rake over every inch of me. He looks *good*, like some damn modern-day pirate in his white button up shirt, the sleeves rolled up on his forearms and the first few buttons undone, the untucked fabric blowing in the light breeze off the water. I watch as he takes a deep, steadying breath, and realize all the air has gone from my lungs. I just stand there, surprise and disbelief holding me in place like an anchor, as he holds both his hands out in front of him. It takes me a moment, but I realize he's holding something in either hand. What is he holding? What is going on?

I look back at Trisha, who has retreated a few steps and seems to be waiting with anticipation for what is about to happen next. I look back at Cam, whose eyes never left the spot where I'm standing.

"What... what is going on?" I ask, finally finding my voice. Cam gulps audibly, before raising his right hand, which I can now see is holding a lighter, and flicks the object with his thumb, eliciting a bright orange flame.

"This is the last item on board that bears the name *Sid's Sea Maiden*," he says, bringing the lighter over to the object in his other hand, a worn piece of paper, and setting it ablaze.

I gasp, taking a few steps back as the flame engulfs the thin piece of paper, still trying to understand what in the world is going on. In just a few short moments, the paper disappears in a small cloud of ash, carried away on the breeze.

"I don't understand," I say, my voice barely above a whisper. Paying my confusion no mind, Cam clears his throat loudly and Eddie pops out from the console, and uncorks a bottle of champagne. The sound echoes throughout the marina, and I look around frantically, noticing that a few people have stopped what they're doing and turned their attention toward Cam's boat. I look from Eddie, to Cam, to Trisha, who just shrugs and grins mischievously. "Seriously, what is going on?" I ask, but Cam continues, undeterred.

He takes the bottle of champagne from Eddie, turns his head toward the sky, and begins to yell at the top of his lungs.

"Poseidon, great and mighty ruler of the seas and oceans! I beg you in your majesty to accept this worthy vessel, and grant her safe passage within your realm!"

My mouth drops open as Cam leans over the stern of the boat, and dumps some of the champagne out into the water. A crowd has begun to gather now, watching with interest and confusion at the commotion coming from Cam's boat. After he's poured a good amount of champagne into the water, he again addresses the sky, raising both of his arms into the air.

"Oh, mighty rulers of the winds! Grant this worth vessel the power and benefit of your bounty!" he yells, before dumping more champagne off of each side of the boat, and finally, it dawns on me what is happening.

Cam is renaming his boat. But why? And why bring me down here for all of this?

After he's done pouring champagne to the North, South, East, and West, Cam hops down off the boat and strides toward me, the audience to the show he's putting on apparently instilling a sense of confidence and determination in him. Eddie follows him off the boat. He stops a few inches from me, still holding the champagne in one hand, and taking my hand in the other.

"Cam, what is all this?" I ask, feeling my heart rate pick up as a sly, sexy smile spreads across his face.

"I'm renaming the boat," he says, very matter-of-factly, as if that explains everything.

"I can see that," I say, recalling our previous conversation about the superstition of renaming boats. He was adamantly against it, insisting that one wrong move could bring untold misfortune. I tilt my head up toward him, entranced by the magnetizing blue of his eyes. "I thought you didn't want to tempt fate."

Cam nods. "It's a risk," he says. "But I realized that some risks are worth taking, even if it means the future is uncertain." He turns to Eddie and nods, who leans down to pull a strip of white covering off the back of the boat. I hadn't even noticed when I first walked up, so distracted by what Cam was doing *on* the boat, that the previous name had been covered. As Eddie begins to peel off the white covering, Cam lifts the champagne in his hand toward the sky one last time, pulling me in close to him.

"With Poseidon's favor, I hereby declare this boat renamed!"

At his words, Eddie tears off the white strip, and I look in awe at the boat's new name, imprinted on the boat in swirly, glossy black lettering.

Second Chance Girl.

The crowd around us erupts in cheers and applause, and Cam takes one last swig of the champagne before turning back to face me. He sets the champagne bottle down and takes my other hand in his, his face suddenly very serious.

"I'm willing to risk whatever bad luck or misfortune might come from renaming the boat," he says, his eyes bearing into mine, right into my very soul. "And I'm willing to risk whatever the future might hold for us, as long as it means I get to be with you. I love you, Lizzie. I always have, and I *always* will. Are you willing to take that risk with me?"

My heart fills with his words, warmth and happiness spreading like a flame through every inch of me as I take in the man in front of me. The man I've loved since I was a teenager. The man I love *now*. The man I honestly never stopped loving. Life might have taken us our separate ways for a time, but it brought us back together for a reason. I knew that the minute I saw him standing in Gran's doorway, that first night back in town. I squeeze his hands tighter, smiling up at him with more love in my heart than I ever thought possible.

"Yes," I say, tears filling my eyes as watch the happiness bloom behind Cam's. "I love you too, Cam. I'm willing to risk it all."

Around us, cheers and applause thunder throughout the marina as Cam wraps his arms around me and claims me with a kiss, letting everyone around us know I am finally, indisputably his.

Epilogue

Cameron

AUGUST, TWO MONTHS Later

"Let me see it! Let me see it!"

Trisha barrels through the small crowd of people in my kitchen, Eddie close at her heels, and grabs Lizzie's hand. She inspects the ring on Lizzie's finger and sighs, the large, princess-cut diamond set in a cushion of small pink diamonds sparkling as Lizzie waggles her finger proudly. Trisha turns to face me.

"You did *great*," she says, holding up Lizzie's hand to show Eddie. "Didn't he do *great?*"

"He did indeed do great," Eddie agrees, giving me a conspiratorial wink.

Within just a few weeks of Lizzie moving back, I had picked out an engagement ring and decided to pop the question one night while watching the sunset on the ocean, snuggled under a blanket on the boat. *Our* boat, now. I figured I'd waited long enough to make Lizzie mine, there was no sense in wasting any more time. Plus, while Helen is hanging in there, her health is still uncertain, and it's important to Lizzie that her grandmother be there for our wedding. We decided a short engagement would be perfect, and we'd plan to get married in the late Fall. Since she doesn't really have any family left besides her grandmother, Lizzie is planning to ask Helen to walk her down the aisle. I have a feeling Helen will be ecstatic.

"Thank you both," Lizzie says, beaming at Trisha and Eddie before turning her adoring gaze toward me. "For everything." The way she looks at me, so full of love and wonder, well... it never gets old, that's for sure.

My mom joins the group, Bella positioned against her chest and shoulder like a newborn, and wraps Lizzie into a hug. "This is a wonderful engagement party," she says, "I'm so happy you'll be a part of this family again. I always knew you and Cam were meant to be, even if he was too *stubborn* to acknowledge it sometimes."

"Hey, this is supposed to be a celebration," I say playfully, wrapping an arm around Lizzie and drawing her in closer to me. "No ragging on the future groom, okay?"

Mom winks at Lizzie. "He hasn't seen anything yet. It's been a while; I think it's time we looked at his baby pictures again. See what a chubby little baby he was," she says, squeezing my cheek. Lizzie just nods emphatically.

"Absolutely," she agrees, blowing me a kiss.

"Traitor," I mutter. My phone vibrates in my pocket and I pull it out, seeing Grayson's name on the screen. He wasn't able to make it out for the party, being as his life in L.A. is... well, let's just say things aren't going very well between him and his co-star-turned-ex-girlfriend. "Excuse me," I say, breaking away from the group to answer the phone.

I find a quiet corner of the house, and hit the *accept* button on my screen "Gray, how's it going?"

"Hey, Cam," he says, forced cheerfulness in his voice. I can tell from his tone that something is wrong.

"What's going on?" I ask, concern for my brother piercing through the excitement and happiness of the day. "Is everything okay?"

"Eh, it could be worse I guess," he says, sighing loudly. "I'm sorry about missing the party."

"Nah, don't be," I say. "As long as you're home for the wedding, that's all I care about."

"Well, about that..."

"Gray, you better get home in time for the wedding," I say, and I can hear Gray chuckling on the other end of the line.

"Chill, dude," he says. "I'll be home in time. I'll actually be home in a couple weeks."

That surprises me. The wedding won't be for another month or so. "A couple weeks? For how long?"

"Well," Gray says, "For as long as it takes for me to figure out what my next career will be. I got fired from the show."

"Shit, Gray," I say, gripping the back of my neck. "That sucks man, I'm sorry."

"Don't be, it's my own fault. Shouldn't have ever dated my co-star. Problem is, I'm like a pariah now. I haven't been able to land a gig in like a month, and I got bills to pay. I'm giving up acting and coming back to Rocky Point."

I'm stunned by Gray's news, considering the last thing I would have ever expected to hear is that's he's giving up and coming back to Rocky Point. "You're giving up on acting? I thought that was your dream job?"

"It's not all it's cracked up to be, it turns out."

"Alright, well, I'm excited to see you. Just sorry it's not under better circumstances."

"All good," Gray says. "But I *do* have a... request."

Typical Gray. "What's that?"

"Can I stay with you? There's no way I can move in with mom, I'll look like a total loser."

"I don't know, man. Lizzie just moved in a few weeks ago, she's putting her Gran's house back up for sale. We're kind of looking forward to... *alone time*, you know?"

"Yuck, I don't want to be stuck in your weird love nest anyway," Gray says, faking a gagging sound. "Fine, I'll move into mom's guest bedroom. But can you keep an eye out for any apartments for rent around town? Living with mom for too long will totally cramp my style in the lady department."

I roll my eyes, even though he can't see me. "I thought you would have learned your lesson by now, Gray. You still planning to break every heart you see when you get back to town?"

"Ah, you know what they say," Gray says. "Once a heartbreaker, always a heartbreaker."

About the Author

Author of contemporary romance, Jessica Thorn brings to life stories full of heart with just enough heat, that tug on your heartstrings, quicken your pulse, and bring a massive smile to your face.
Follow her on Facebook at:
https://www.facebook.com/jessicathornbooks
Visit her website at www.jessicathornbooks.com
To stay up to date on new releases and get exclusive author content, subscribe to her newsletter at:
https://jessicathornbooks.ck.page/bc03070198